Medics .... *es*

When it comes to fulfilling their duties, these heroes and heroines are at the top of their game, but when it comes to love, their successes are much more limited! Career driven and ambitious, it's a shock to them all when love sneaks up and threatens to blow apart their carefully formed plans...

Discover their stories in this fabulous new duet by Charlotte Hawkes.

Second Chance with His Army Doc

Company Sergeant Major Kane Wheeler has a lot to apologize to army doc Major Mattie Brigham for. He broke both of their hearts when he walked out on their relationship, but now fate—and the British Army—has given him the chance to make things right!

Reawakened by Her Army Major

It was only supposed to be a one-night fling— working together in extreme conditions means that Major Hayden Brigham and nurse Bridget Gardiner need to keep their hands firmly off each other, but when the boundaries between desire and duty begin to blur, love might triumph!

Dear Reader,

Before I even came up with the idea of an army duet, the characters of Hayden "Hayd" Brigham and Mathilda "Mattie" Brigham were patrolling around my head. Two siblings with a brigadier father, who competed with each other to be the best soldier, but who always loved each other and would always have each other's backs.

I knew they would both need strong, independent individuals to counterbalance them.

For Hayden, that's Bridget Gardiner, a woman who seems socially shy in the real world but who shocks him with her steely will and determination out in hostile environments. He finds her so different to any other woman he's ever known before.

Yet even as I was writing their story, I found it fun to see how hard I had to work to convince my characters to do what I wanted. In particular, Bridget couldn't seem to see what I could see— that she was just the right woman to slip behind Hayden's armor and find the side of him that he usually kept hidden! I hope you have as much fun reading their story as I had writing it.

Charlotte x

REAWAKENED BY HER ARMY MAJOR

—

CHARLOTTE HAWKES

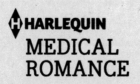

HARLEQUIN

MEDICAL
ROMANCE

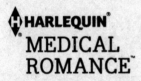

HARLEQUIN®
MEDICAL
ROMANCE™

Recycling programs
for this product may
not exist in your area.

ISBN-13: 978-1-335-14968-8

Reawakened by Her Army Major

Copyright © 2020 by Charlotte Hawkes

This edition published by arrangement with Harlequin Books S.A.

For questions and comments about the quality of this book,
please contact us at CustomerService@Harlequin.com.

Harlequin Enterprises ULC
22 Adelaide St. West, 40th Floor
Toronto, Ontario M5H 4E3, Canada
www.Harlequin.com

Printed in U.S.A.

Born and raised on the Wirral Peninsula in England, **Charlotte Hawkes** is mom to two intrepid boys who love her to play building block games with them, and who object loudly to the amount of time she spends on the computer. When she isn't writing—or building with blocks—she is company director for a small Anglo/French construction firm. Charlotte loves to hear from readers, and you can contact her at her website: charlotte-hawkes.com.

Books by Charlotte Hawkes

Harlequin Medical Romance

A Summer in São Paolo

Falling for the Single Dad Surgeon

Hot Army Docs

Encounter with a Commanding Officer
Tempted by Dr. Off-Limits

The Army Doc's Secret Wife
The Surgeon's Baby Surprise
A Bride to Redeem Him
The Surgeon's One-Night Baby
Christmas with Her Bodyguard
A Surgeon for the Single Mom
The Army Doc's Baby Secret
Unwrapping the Neurosurgeon's Heart
Surprise Baby for the Billionaire

Visit the Author Profile page at Harlequin.com.

To Vic.

Thank you for being such a fab—
and patient—editor! xx

**Praise for
Charlotte Hawkes**

"Overall, Ms. Hawkes has delivered a really good
read in this book where I smiled a lot because of the
growing relationship between the hero and heroine…
The romance was well worth the wait because of the
building sexual tension between the pair."

—*Harlequin Junkie* on
A Surgeon for the Single Mom

CHAPTER ONE

'RELAX, BEA, YOU look great.'

Stopping outside the doors to the nightclub, where a muffled bass beat was already audible, Bridget Gardiner smoothed down the shimmery short dress she'd borrowed from her friend and tried not to look awkward or out of place.

Not feel like some scraggly stray next to the strikingly sophisticated Mattie Brigham.

'You're sure?' Bridget shifted uncertainly.

'I'm definitely sure. Perfect for finally breaking out of your shell and trying something a little bit crazy.'

'Yeah…about that…'

'Oh, no. You can't back out now, Bea. Weren't you the one who originally said that tonight was about having fun?'

'Yes…' Bridget trailed off uncertainly.

Tonight *was* supposed to be about fun. Only *wanting* to do something crazy and actually *doing* something crazy were two very separate things.

'Weren't you also the one who said that we spend most of our careers being serious?' Mattie continued. '*Too* serious sometimes. Tonight is about just cutting loose, right?'

'I know…'

'Got to take a few chances. Life's too short not to. Trust me.'

Bridget eyed her friend for a moment. She couldn't put her finger on it, but Mattie seemed different tonight. Perhaps a little…agitated? Not obviously so, just flashes every now and then. Certainly not the cool, collected army major and doctor that Bridget was accustomed to seeing.

'Everything okay, Mattie?'

Mattie hesitated and, for a moment Bridget thought she was going to say something. But then her friend seemed to pull her shoulders back and roll her eyes.

'Ghosts from the past.' She shrugged, back to her usual self. On the outside at least. 'Gotta shake them off. Maybe I should try something crazy too, just so you're not alone.'

'It's fine.' Bridget plastered a bright smile on her face and tried to look earnest. 'Actually, I'm looking forward to tonight.'

'Liar!' Mattie laughed softly, reaching for the door handle and pulling it open as the thrum of music spilled out into the street. 'I know you'd be ten times more at home in some aid post in a disaster area. And a hundred times more confident. You can handle rebels and guerrillas in the middle of some refugee camp thousands of miles from home, Bea.'

'You make me sound a lot cooler than I really am…' Bridget wrinkled her nose.

'You *are* cool, Bea. But the fact that you're practically quaking at the idea of meeting a bunch of my army buddies, not to mention my thorn-in-my-side big brother, *isn't* so cool. In fact, it's daft.'

'I know that, too,' Bridget admitted.

Although, to be fair, it was meeting Hayden that was worrying her most. Mattie might grumble about her brother—also an army officer—but there was absolutely no mistaking the fact that she loved him without reservation. How many times had she lamented the fact that their respective army careers meant they didn't see each other—or their retired army brigadier father—enough?

And then, as if on cue, the doubts began creeping in. As familiar and painful as ever.

Bridget gritted her teeth and tried to shut them out, but it was impossible.

What if Hayden didn't like her? What if he told Mattie that she wasn't good enough to be Mattie's friend?

Stop it, you're not fourteen any more.

She wasn't *that kid* who all the cool kids

pointed at and laughed at. The one whose father was a fraudster and a conman.

'Good. So, *fun*,' Mattie said firmly, oblivious to the sudden turmoil in Bridget's mind. 'Good, clean fun. Then back to the serious stuff tomorrow, okay?'

'Okay.' Bridget paused then returned Mattie's gentle smile with a rather sheepish one of her own. 'I'm ready.'

'Still a lie, but more convincing.' Mattie grinned. 'Trust me, Bea, we've been through this, they're a nice bunch and they'll love you.'

With that, her friend ducked into the club, leaving Bridget to follow, coming to an abrupt halt for a moment as a heavy wall of heat and sound hit her with such a wallop that for a moment she forgot how to breathe.

She watched Mattie accept the two proffered welcome jelly shots from the girl at the door, then let her friend place one in her hand.

'Open your mouth, pinch the container, and swallow.' Mattie demonstrated. 'Wow. Now, they *are* strong!'

Closing her eyes and sending out a silent prayer, Bridget followed suit. It slid down her throat surprisingly smoothly, the taste sweet but with a kick nonetheless. Then Mattie grabbed her hand and plunged them both into the gyrating bodies.

Like Alice down the rabbit hole.

And whether it was the crowd, the music or the insanely strong shot, Bridget found her body heating up and her brain beginning to loosen its grip just a fraction. People bumped her—or perhaps she bumped them—and swept her along, as if her feet weren't always quite touching the ground.

She was almost grateful when Mattie came to a stop in front of a small, friendly looking group who erupted into shouts and laughs, all of them jostling a little in their obvious eagerness to greet their friend. And before she realised it, they were turning to acknowledge her, too. Warmly, but not too over the top. Mattie had been right, her friends were a nice bunch, and this was actually...*fun.*

Right up until the moment when Mattie gave a low cry and hurled herself past Bridget.

'Hayd. You're here.'

Bridget turned, amused, but instead something jolted through her. Like a shock of electricity. Her body didn't even feel like her own any longer or, if it did, she certainly didn't have any control over it. Instead, all she could do was stand there, frozen in place like one of her teenage nightmares, her eyes struggling to refocus. To take it all in.

So, this was Mattie's brother, the infamous Major Hayden Brigham. He wasn't at all how she'd pictured him.

Then again, she wasn't sure *how* she'd pictured him. Good looking, certainly, since Mattie had never made any bones about that fact, but Bridget had put it down to indulgence on the part of a loving sister. Hayden was apparently a very eligible bachelor—and what was more, he knew it—so he didn't sound at all her type. If she actually *had* a type, that was. Still, she'd thought she'd been fully prepared for meeting him in person.

But she'd been wrong. In truth, surely nothing could have prepared any woman for the reality of meeting the guy in person.

He wasn't just good looking—such a description was too pedestrian for a man like Major Hayden Brigham. He was…arresting—*magnificent*—and if there was a perfect specimen of male beauty, it was him.

Less of a man, more of a mountain, yet unequivocally male. Bridget was fairly certain she heard a collective sigh of appreciation from the female contingent of the entire club. Or maybe that was just her?

And she hated herself for it. It was so *not* her to lust over a man. *Any* man. But certainly not one who was also the brother of the closest thing Bridget had had to a best friend since she'd been a kid. Certainly not one with whom she was going to be working—out in the middle of nowhere on the African continent—for the next three months.

Well, not *working with* exactly. But close enough. Which was why, no matter how insane her body was going right now, she *didn't* fancy him. She refused to.

Yet what was to be done when everything about him, from that crop of short yet deliciously tousled dirty-blond hair down to the jaw—so square that a carpenter could have used it to take perfect right angles—was stunning? Not to mention those Baltic-blue eyes that seemed to peer into her very soul, holding her own and making it feel as though her entire face was on fire.

She couldn't move, could barely even breathe. She had no idea how she managed to wrest her gaze away, but suddenly it was dropping. Down over those broad, strong shoulders to which the fitted shirt clung so lovingly, and did absolutely nothing to disguise, and over the indisputably defined chest as it tapered to the sexiest set of male hips she imagined had ever existed.

She couldn't look down any further. She didn't dare. And so they lingered there—shamefully—somewhere around his belt buckle.

Fleetingly, Bridget considered making her escape. Rushing for the Ladies' to douse herself with some much-needed cold water. Naturally, it was that exact moment that her friend chose to introduce the two of them.

'Bridget, this is my brother, Hayden. Hayd, meet Bridget Gardiner, who I've been telling you about. Though she's off limits, right?'

More heat—if it was even possible—rushed to Bridget's face, even as her mouth became too parched to begin to respond. Not that it mattered, as Hayden was already speaking, his rich, deep, yet slightly wry tone doing…*things* to Bridget's insides.

She needed to get a grip. Draw on some of that strength she always had in one of those refugee camps in the middle of some foreign country.

'Thank you, Mattie…' the low, rich voice rolled through her, despite the deep pulse of the nightclub bass line, leaving her altogether too… *aware* of her own body '…for making it sound as though I pounce on every friend you introduce me to. And, Bridget, I've heard a fair bit about you, It's a pleasure.'

He held his hand out, the movement breaking her stare, and she snapped her eyes back up in an instant.

His blue eyes glittered. All-knowing. Clearly amused.

Her flush intensified as she thrust out her hand to his proffered one, shaking it clumsily. She'd never, *never* reacted to anyone like this. She'd thought it was something reserved for films, or books. But, lord, how Hayden positively *oozed* authority. And power.

It was…intoxicating.

You can resist him. You can resist him… Bridget began to chant it furiously to herself, like some kind of new mantra.

As if she would actually need to try.

As if Hayden would even look twice at a woman so quiet that she could make wallflowers look like prima donnas.

But, then, that was what happened when you'd spent the first thirteen years of your life gliding around the most glittering, monied, social circles, only for absolutely everything to tumble down in the most shameful way when your father had got arrested for fraud.

Was it any wonder, then, Bridget thought, not for the first time, that she'd spent the next thirteen years making herself as inconsequential and invisible as possible, fighting to shake off those associations?

Only now, right at this minute, standing in the spotlight of Hayden's stare, she didn't feel inconsequential or invisible, or gawky and out of step. Instead, she felt raw. Wobbly. Naked.

And a raft of other things she couldn't—or didn't want to—identify.

Get a grip.

'Hayden.' Thrusting her hand out to take his proffered one, she wasn't prepared for the jolt of electricity that zapped right through her, from the tips of her fingers right to her core. Right…

there. Bridget was frankly astounded that she managed to make her voice sound remotely normal. 'Likewise.'

'Call me Hayd. Everyone does.'

Hayd. Even his name sang a new song inside Bridget's head. It should have been laughable but instead, shamefully, she found that she was entranced.

'I don't think you pounce on every friend I introduce to you,' Mattie's firm, all-too-shrewd voice cut in. 'Just those who have something about them.'

'I take it she's always this complimentary about me?' Hayden... *Hayd* turned to Bridget with raised eyebrows, but the twitch of his mouth was almost mesmerising.

It was all she could do not to let her legs crumple. They were certainly shaky enough.

'Incredible brother, amazing commanding officer, but unashamed playboy.' She ticked off each trait on one hand, as if entirely amused and not the least bit affected.

'Playboy?' He frowned.

'Well, not those words exactly,' Bridget confessed.

Though she'd added the *playboy* bit to keep her own head screwed on, if nothing else. How he couldn't hear the deafening hammering of her heart was mystifying, though perhaps he was altogether too accustomed to it.

'I think it was more *women always throwing themselves at his feet.* But I get the impression you're not exactly a monk.'

'He definitely isn't a monk.' Mattie clicked her tongue. 'Are you okay for a minute, Bea? I ought to say hi to everyone.'

How was it possible to simultaneously want to grab her friend's arm and make her stay, and yet to push her on her way and tell her not to rush back?

'Sure.' She managed to smile instead, though it felt like a rictus.

'I'll take care of her.' Hayden's voice sent goosebumps chasing up her skin.

'Yeah, well, not *too* much care.' Mattie skewered him with a glower before bestowing a smile on Bridget. 'He's not what I meant by doing something crazy.'

'Of course not,' Bridget agreed, wondering why her voice sounded so robotic. And then Mattie was gone, and she was left alone with her friend's brother. And her body launched itself into another insane fever.

What was the matter with her?

Hayden Brigham was positively lethal and according to Mattie any woman worth her salt should steer clear of the man, or at least be able to steel herself against his natural charms.

She'd been confident she'd fall easily into that category. Now she feared for her own sanity. Less than three minutes in this man's company and her body was already feeling out of her control, and alien. What would three months of working with him be like?

'Something *crazy*?' he echoed, and for a moment she couldn't be sure if it was a question or an invitation.

Bridget stuffed down the sudden thrill that rose within her and told herself it was entirely unwelcome.

She didn't believe in that stuff. *Love, lust, sex*, whatever one wanted to call it. She'd seen first-hand how destructive that could be. How her father had used her mother's love for him, and her gullibility, to defend him. To lie for him. All because she had refused to believe what was right in front of her eyes.

Such was the power he'd had over her mother that for years she'd made Bridget—too young to know any better—lie for him, too. And as Bridget had grown up and had seen for herself what kind of a smooth-talking con artist her father was, she had assured herself that she simply couldn't see how anyone could be that naive.

Right now, however, she was terribly afraid she could begin to understand all too easily. Not that she was saying Hayden Brigham was anything like her father, of course…just that it was suddenly all too easy to see how one could succumb to someone with boundless charisma and incredible looks.

'Never mind,' she managed to choke out quietly, before raising her voice. 'I've heard a lot about you.'

'Judging by my sister's comments, I'm not altogether convinced that's a good thing.' His lips twitched in amusement and Bridget found herself helplessly bewitched. 'Let me assure you that whilst whatever I do in my downtime is my business, I am strictly professional when it comes to operations or exercises.'

'Right,' Bridget muttered.

And what did it say about her that a hint of disappointment rippled through her at Hayden's reassurance? Or that his gaze slid lazily over her as though he could read her reaction in every line of her body.

'Relax, no need to be nervous.'

'I'm not,' she lied, silently trying to bolster herself.

'Is that so? Your shaking hands say otherwise but, trust me, I won't bite.'

'Not unless I want you to—isn't that how the saying goes?' The quip was out before she even realised what she was saying.

Something pulled sharply in his gaze, but Bridget couldn't even begin to read it. She was too horrified at herself.

'I'm sorry... I don't...'

'And here I was, under strict instructions from Mattie that that's exactly the sort of remark I'm not allowed to make.'

He was laughing at her, and she couldn't blame him. Still, she prickled uncomfortably.

'I apologise unreservedly, Hayden,' she began. 'That really isn't the—'

'Hayd,' he reminded her, and she faltered uncertainly.

'Seriously, no one really calls me Hayden except my father, and the general if he isn't happy with me. Although I admit that doesn't happen often.'

Out of all the questions and responses swirling around her head, it was inconceivable that the one she came out with was, 'Isn't that a little arrogant?'

'No. Just factual.' He shrugged, but that smile still toyed with his lips.

A mouth that was more sinfully tempting than Bridget could ever have thought possible.

What was happening here?

'Are you always so...*factual*?'

'It depends on the subject, I suppose. But, yes, I try to be. I prefer that to people saying things they don't really mean.'

'I prefer that, too,' she said, before she realised she was even speaking.

'Yes. I think that's one of the reasons why my sister has taken to you so well.'

'Mattie has talked about me?' Surprise bounced through her. 'To you?'

His eyes skated over her face, leaving Bridget with the distinct impression that he was able to read altogether too much, just from her face. She tried to smooth out her features into whatever might pass for a passive or neutral expression. But that only seemed to elicit a ghost of a smile from his wickedly tempting mouth.

'She said you've been working for the charity for years. From Chad to South Sudan, in outreach clinics and major foreign aid hospitals alike.'

'I first met her after the earthquakes in Nepal,' Bridget heard herself say. 'I was a nurse for an NGO, and Mattie's army medical unit had come to help because of the sheer scale of the disaster.'

'Yeah, I remember her saying you were with the medical charity already on site. You and she dragged all the patients into the street when an aftershock ripped through the hospital building?'

'In a nutshell,' Bridget agreed, surprised he knew.

Even now, she could remember the moment with such clarity. The shock had rocked the buildings they'd been using as a temporary medical facility, some of the ceilings had fallen in with the intensity, and even the walls had shown signs of crumbling. If she closed her eyes, Bridget could still hear the shouts and screams in the streets.

She remembered looking for the patients she knew were the most severely injured, just as Mattie had taken charge, quickly and calmly instructing not just her army medics but *all* the staff. Determining that it was no longer safe to treat them indoors and designating the order that the patients needed to be stretchered outside, even as she sent a recce team to find a safe location and begin to set up large tents and temporary beds.

At that moment she'd seen Mattie as a mentor. A woman who might only be a few years older than she herself was but who was years ahead in terms of her career. A woman whose unique attitude had allowed her to easily adapt from being commanding officer to empathetic doctor—exactly the kind of doctor that Bridget had once hoped that she herself might have become, if things had been different.

If only her father's suicide following his arrest hadn't left her already fragile-minded mother a wreck, needing to be taken care of, leaving Bridget no room for studies or a career. Not that anything she'd done had ever been good enough for her mother.

Not until her mother had finally met a new man to fill that obvious void in her life and make her feel complete. And then Bridget had finally been able to start making a life for herself. First as a nurse and then as a volunteer for foreign aid charities in the hope that one day one would sponsor her to finally realise her dream and become a doctor.

If only her life had been different.

But it hadn't been. Bridget steeled herself as she had so many other times when her mind had threatened to take a little detour down this particular memory lane. What was the point thinking about something she could never change?

'So now I'm going to be working with another Brigham sibling.' She managed a laugh, trying to divert her mind. 'You're a major in the Royal Engineers?'

CHAPTER TWO

'I AM.' HE GRINNED, and she had to steel her legs from going as jelly-like as the shot she'd had when she'd walked into the club.

It was surely *that* which was making her feel so…*odd.*

'How does that work?'

'Your charity is working in a camp, providing medical aid, yes?'

'Camp Jukrem,' she confirmed. 'The country has been through decades of civil war, and now it's over they need to get back on their feet. We're there to help them with medical aid, water, sanitation, supplies. But the peace is new. Fragile.'

'Which is exactly why the new government decided to rent a some of its land to the British Army as a training ground, about a thousand square miles of it.'

'That's quite significant.' Bridget emitted a low whistle, which was easily absorbed in the noise of the club.

'Yeah, it's a twenty-five-year agreement that

gives the new country's fledgling government money to start the rebuilding process. In addition, our presence should help to deter any unrest, and as part of our use of the land we'll be putting in infrastructure for them. Roads, bridges, buildings.'

'So you chose to come to Jukrem?'

'Actually, I understand your charity has camps all over the region, but they set up Jukrem once they knew we were starting from that point. They asked us to work in conjunction with them.'

'I hadn't realised that,' Bridget admitted, 'but it makes sense. Jukrem is the furthest south we've ever gone—usually the area gets hit by the rains, and roads and airstrips get washed out. If the British Army is there, putting in bridges, we'll be able to reach refugees who might never get to any of our camps further north.'

'So what was the last project you worked on?' he asked.

'The last one was a TB facility. Part of it was for treating *normal* tuberculosis, for want of a better term, but the other side had a village for patients suffering from a drug-resistant strain of TB.'

He drew his eyebrows together, and she had to clench her fingers to resist the urge to reach out and smooth his forehead.

'I thought TB could be cured with antibiotics. How does a strain become drug-resistant?'

'Do you really want to know, or are you try-ing to be polite?' She pulled a wry face, only too conscious of the fact that he'd touched on a topic that bubbled inside her. 'Only we're meant to be here to celebrate Mattie's promotion.'

Despite all her usual social awkwardness, her job was a subject about which she could chat to anyone, any time. It was more than just a job, it was a passion, and she loved being out there, helping people who wouldn't have had anything otherwise.

'Is it something we're likely to encounter where we're going?' he asked, and she liked it that he seemed to have actually taken a moment to think about his answer.

'It is,' she confirmed. 'The fact is that TB thrives in communities that live very close to-gether, and where their immune systems are al-ready weakened. We're heading into an area where there are refugees and displaced persons with no homes, no access to fresh water, and who will be malnourished. Their immune sys-tems would already be in the toilet, if it weren't for the fact that the sanitation will be poor, too.'

He laughed. A deep throaty sound that made her feel insanely good about her attempt at hu-mour. Like he found her fun, and amusing. Mostly people found her too serious back here in the UK. It was strange how she felt like a dif-ferent person as soon as she stepped out of that plane in a foreign country, ready for her next medical mission. Freer, and more *herself* than she had ever felt back here.

'There you go, then. I'm genuinely interested.' Hayden stepped closer, making something surge inside her, even as she told herself it was just so they could hear each other better. 'I've spent almost half my life as an officer in the army, I've completed multiple tours in war zones, and I've been part of hearts and minds missions before. But this is the first time I've ever been part of one quite like this. I'm curious to know what to expect and I think you're the perfect person to tell me.'

'I don't want to bore you,' Bridget said.

It was the truth, but without the inconvenient fact that a part of her wished she was the kind of sexy, confident woman who could hold a guy's attention without having to resort to conversations about what, halfway around the world, they called sputum positives.

'Besides…' he grinned, as if reading her mind '… I can't say I'm much of a club-goer. I wouldn't even be here if this wasn't about the only time all our group had downtime at the same time. At least teach me something to make my night feel less wasted.'

He was teasing her. She knew it, and his words rolled through her, making heat bloom wherever they went. Making her feel *interesting*.

'Okay,' she began, unable to help herself. 'You want to know about drug-resistant TB, or XDR TB, as we call it. So buckle up.'

'Consider me warned.' His eyes glittered with amusement, though Bridget didn't realise she'd been staring into the deep blue pools until she ran out of breath and realised she'd forgotten to keep breathing.

'We've been running TB clinics out in places like Jukrem camp for years. The main problem we face is that treating TB usually takes about six months in normal conditions, and necessitates oral drugs and daily injections.' She pulled a wry face. '*Painful* injections. You have no idea how long I spent on my first mission, thinking that the local people were particularly susceptible to hip or leg bone problems, only to discover they were in pain from the injections they had to have in their bottoms.'

'Ah.' Hayden winced in empathy, and she liked it that he seemed to get it.

'They're confined to small wards or mud huts, and can't really mix with others. Often they've been separated from family. All too frequently, they leave before their treatment course is complete.'

'I'm beginning to see where you're going.' He raised his eyebrows. 'If they leave before they should then they won't be fully cured, but their body will have been exposed to the drugs and begun to build up resistance.'

It had to be the least sexy conversation in the club, and yet she could have kissed him for making her feel so engaging.

She ignored the voice in her head telling her that she could have kissed him for a very different reason, too.

'Right,' she continued, dragging her mind back to the infinitely less sexy conversation. 'So, we end up with a patient who comes back to us later, having developed XDR TB. As it is, we often get an all-clear patient returning home, only to be reinfected by a family member who hadn't yet been treated, or even screened, for TB. But the worst thing about XDR TB is that it can be spread the same way. So suddenly we get swathes of villages or cities that *all* have the drug-resistant strain, and there's very little we can do about it.'

'You're passionate about this, aren't you?' Hayden said suddenly, making her blink as she met his gaze.

'It sounds silly, doesn't it?' she noted, her voice flat even to her own ears.

'It doesn't sound remotely silly. It sounds like you care about other people and about trying to do what's best for them. And it sounds like you love your career, which is something I, of all people, can truly understand.'

Bridget didn't answer, she could only jerk her head awkwardly up and down, entranced by the quiet intensity in his eyes. As though they were forging some kind of bond. Here. In the middle of a nightclub.

And it was suddenly inexplicably important to her that Hayden see her not as a socially awkward wallflower but as the confident, competent woman he would be working with over the next few months.

Is that all it is?

She stamped the needling voice out quickly, scrabbling around for something to divert her and falling back on the safety of their previous conversation.

'It's hard sometimes,' she heard herself admitting. 'Especially when it's a husband and wife where the wife is afraid to sleep away from her husband, but they need to because one of them is entering an intensive phase of their treatment. And they may only live in a one-room hut or shed.'

'So what do you do?'

'Talk to them. Try to explain.' She lifted her shoulders slightly. 'But sometimes the best thing you can do is just find a hospital room where they can be at opposite ends but see each other. And where there are plenty of windows in between.'

'It's a fine balance.' He smiled gently, and it tugged at her. Hard.

Again she floundered for some kind of response.

'It is,' she managed, before fading out awkwardly.

This time, she knew, the conversation had reached its natural conclusion.

Bridget braced herself, mentally preparing for him to turn away and strike up a conversation with someone less...*serious*. More alluring.

'So you're Bridget,' he continued smoothly, not moving away even a fraction, she noted. 'But you prefer Bea?'

'Actually, I don't really,' she heard herself admit out of nowhere.

Hayden frowned.

'I thought that's what my sister calls you?'

'It is.' Bridget pulled a wry face, not really understanding what had come over her. 'I've never really liked being called Bea, but... I never told her.'

'I see,' he noted, and she wondered what it was that he was filing away for later. 'What about Birdie?'

It walloped her out of the blue. For a moment she wasn't sure her lungs would even kick back into gear.

'Birdie,' she whispered, too softly for him to hear over the music.

'No? Just Bridget, then?'

It was odd, this wistful sensation that suddenly wound around her.

'Birdie's what I used to be called as a kid.'

By her father before…everything. She'd loved that name, but then he'd tainted it somehow.

'Right.'

She was dimly aware that Hayden was watching her, but she couldn't quite bring herself to focus.

'You used to like it? Or dislike it?'

'I loved it,' she admitted, ignoring the fact that no one had called her that since the day her father had taken his own life.

And the fact that she'd never wanted them to.

'Birdie it is, then.' Hayden's voice unfurled through her, low, edgy and hot.

And then he flashed her a smile that was surely so maddeningly dazzling that it could have caused a major power outage in any city. Every caution in her head evaporated in a puff of smoke.

Birdie—she liked the way it rolled off Hayden's tongue.

Snapping her eyes to his, she tilted her chin up, feeling a long-lost surge of confidence. It reminded her of the way she'd used to be— once, long ago. Spirited and happy, bold and fun-loving. The way she only ever felt these days when she was thousands of miles away from the place she called home. Yet this relative stranger—the playboy brother of her friend and mentor—was making her feel that same boldness right now.

More than that, he was making her feel alive in a way she wasn't sure she'd ever felt before. Making her body feel as though it was waking up from a slumber she hadn't known she was in.

How was that even possible?

If she didn't get a handle on these unchecked, uncharacteristic emotions, she was going to make a fool of herself with this man before she'd even got out to Jukrem camp. And then how would they be able to work well together?

What the hell was he playing at?

Flirting with Bridget Gardiner was a distinctly bad idea, and not just because his sister would rip him a new one.

He knew a bit about Bridget from Mattie and, from everything his sister had told him, he'd been expecting her friend to be a sweet, shy, pretty in an unobtrusive girl-next-door kind of way. Someone who was unequivocally too innocent and saintly for the likes of him, which was good as he was rather more partial to a bit more of a sinner.

Yet what had smacked him across the face the moment he'd been introduced to Bridget had been that there was nothing *saintly* about her at all. Nothing *unobtrusive* and nothing low-key. Rather, Bridget Gardiner looked very much like she was a sex symbol stepping right out of the nineteen-fifties or -sixties.

And his body had ached on sight.

A figure-hugging dress moulded itself around her, as though she'd had to be poured into it, encasing generous breasts that made his palms long to cup them, a tapered waist that made his fingers itch to span it, and slinky hips that made his entire body hunger to press up against them.

It was all so ridiculously...*adolescent* of him.

He was never this out of control. He tried concentrating on her face, but that didn't help at all. His mouth felt parched even as his eyes drank her in like she was the longest, coolest drink he'd ever had. He didn't know if it was her large, dark eyes with their slightly startled expression, the pretty oval face framed by the mass of thick, glossy black hair, or the sultry pout that Hayden didn't think she was even aware of. And as for that tiny but deliciously naughty gap between her front teeth...he wanted to lower his mouth to hers right now and taste it.

Forcing himself to take a step back, Hayden folded his arms over his chest as if it could help him resist this unexpected pull that this woman had over him. This couldn't happen. It was wrong.

He was about to spend three months working

alongside her in the middle of nowhere, thousands of miles from anywhere. And the fact that she was clearly so damned passionate about her work only appealed to him all the more. Yet having a fling with her would be worse than simply a *bad* idea, it would be a downright *catastrophic* idea.

As much as he had a reputation—not entirely fair since he wasn't anywhere as indiscriminate as he knew rumour painted him, although he would freely admit that he was no monk—he had a strict rule about not mixing professional with personal.

Only right now, at this instant, his head was wrecked and his body was in the process of ripping up the rule book and hurling it out of the window. If he didn't retake the reins on what little self-control he had remaining, he feared he was going to lose his grip completely. And then…well, he'd have three months in the middle of nowhere with a woman who would want more from him and be hurt and upset that he couldn't give that to her.

Not to mention a sister who would rip seven shades out of him for devasting her friend.

It might not seem like it now, faced with all the temptations of that luscious body, but it really wasn't worth the hassle.

'Your champagne, sir?'

Hayden blinked as the bartender approached

them, several bottles in a couple of buckets of ice, along with enough flutes to go around. It took him a moment to recall that he'd ordered them earlier because they were all here to celebrate his sister's promotion. A fact he appeared to have forgotten in the event of meeting Bridget, despite her mentioning it earlier.

He didn't care to analyse why it was that he both welcomed and resented the intrusion at the same time.

'Do you always drink champagne in night-clubs?'

'Not exactly,' he told her, taking the magnums and setting them down. 'We don't usually do either. But tonight we're celebrating something big for Mattie. And sometimes it's good to cut loose, especially after a hard tour. Or before one. Plus, it's not often we're all in the same place like this, but with the RAF base down the road and all of us here at the same time, even if we are flying out to different locations, it seemed like the perfect time.'

Bridget didn't answer, and Hayden turned back to see her staring at the bottles with an expression he could only describe as agonised.

'Birdie?'

She didn't react, and before he could stop himself he reached out to gently take her chin in his fingers and tilt her head up to him.

He pretended he didn't feel the sparks that arced between them.

She startled, freezing for a moment before wrenching her head away, muttering as she did so, 'It's nothing.'

It was a patent lie and he shouldn't want so badly to call her out on it. What did it matter to him if she told him the truth or not?

'Excuse me, please.' He turned away to stop himself from pressing Bridget any further when she clearly didn't want to talk and picked up a bottle before deftly popping the cork.

'How did you do that?' she asked suddenly, touching her hand to the inside of his wrist until he opened his hand and she picked up the cork. 'I had visions of it flying across the room.'

He told himself that his pulse wasn't leaping at the contact. That it wasn't the reason why he'd forgotten to pour the champagne into the first flute and it was now effervescing over the top.

Hastily, he remedied the situation and set the bottle down where one of his and Mattie's mutual friends picked it up, telling him they'd pour if he opened. But his attention was on Bridget, whether he liked it or not.

'The trick's in the wrist,' he told her, taking the second bottle. 'You take the bottle in one hand and hold the cork with the other, like this. Now hold the cork steady and twist the bottle.'

It made a distinct pop as it opened, and this

time Hayden reached for a flute to pour out the first bit before setting it on the table as before. He took the last bottle and held it out to her.

'You try.'

She eyed it for a moment, her body language revealing how tempted she was. But instead she shook her head.

'I might drop it.'

'It's all a matter of confidence.' He smiled.

She hesitated, but ultimately shook her head again.

'Want me to show you?' He knew it was a bad idea, but the words tumbled out all the same.

She slid him a curious look.

'How?'

Hayden didn't give himself chance to rethink the wisdom of what he knew was damn fool idea when he reached out and placed his hands on Bridget's hips, spinning her round as he stepped behind her and circled his arms around her to bring the champagne bottle to her front.

'Are you left- or right-handed?'

She didn't answer at first, her body tense, like something was coiled inside her, ready to run.'

'It's just opening a champagne bottle, Birdie,' he murmured.

Only…it wasn't *just* that, was it? He was lying to himself if he thought it was. He was complicating an already problematic situation. In a matter of days they would be working together and it was like he didn't even care. All he could think about was the heat of her back against his chest, the feel of her trembling slightly in his arms, and the faint vanilla scent pervading his nostrils.

'Now, hold the bottle here...' he lifted her hand, covering it with his own '...and put the other hand on the cork. Good, okay. Hold the cork in place without moving that hand and slowly turn the bottle with the other.'

In one easy movement the cork popped.

'Well done,' Hayden told her, stepping away as he reached for a flute.

But the damage was done. He was more intrigued than ever—or at least his body was. He wanted her. So badly that he could feel need advancing through him like an infantry unit on a forced march. If this is where he was after a few minutes on a night out with Bridget, how would it be after a few hours? With dancing? And the added headache of alcohol?

It all made for a distinctly potent cocktail. That meant the wisest course of action would be to abstain. He would stay long enough to toast Mattie, and then, when she went to buy a round of drinks as per tradition, he would make his excuses and leave.

It was the right thing to do. The responsible thing.

Before he was tempted to do anything he would regret with the delectable Bridget.

CHAPTER THREE

BRIDGET WAS STILL shaking as Hayden stepped away and prepared to toast his sister.

Never, in her entire life, had anyone affected her this much. This badly. He'd been so careful not to actually let their bodies make contact and yet she'd felt him everywhere. *Everywhere*.

It had started with a delicious tingling at her hairline, whether from his breath on her skin or just the simple fact that he'd been so close she had no idea. Then, as he'd closed his arms around her, a wave of tiny goosebumps had swept over her entire body. Her breasts had felt a sudden heaviness, her nipples pulling tighter than she'd ever known. But it had been the ache inside her that had scared her the most. Pulsing right through her body. Pooling right *there*.

The softest, hottest part of her. Where she longed for Hayden—this virtual stranger—to touch her. And it terrified her. She had never, *never*, craved something so much.

It had taken all she had not to edge back into

Hayden's arms and press her body up against his. To find out if he wanted her anywhere near as much as her body seemed to be screaming out for him.

Like it knew things that her inexperienced brain didn't understand. All she did know for sure was that she needed to stay far, far away from this dark, greedy thing that was winding its way up inside her.

She needed to stay away from Hayden.

Taking a proffered champagne flute, she backed away until she was on the other side of the gathering, all the while acutely conscious that his eyes were on her. Tracking her.

And then he moved his gaze to the group, that dazzling smile back on his face, leaving her feel oddly bereft.

'My little sister, Major Mathilda Brigham, soon to be Lieutenant-Colonel Mathilda Brigham.' Hayden raised his glass at last, ensuring his voice could be heard over the deep pulse of the nightclub bass line. 'To Mattie.'

'To Mattie,' the handful of friends echoed.

As the group began to split, Bridget watched Hayden chatting proudly to his sister, unable to drag her gaze from his profile. What was it about him that captivated her most? she wondered. Was it as simple as the stark beauty of his physique, or was it more the way he held himself, or the ease of his body language? She couldn't work it out.

She was still staring when a shadow fell across her vision moments before one of the other guys in the group stepped in front of her. Effectively blocking off her self-indulgent ogling.

'Bridget, isn't it?'

It took her a moment to pull herself together.

'Yes.' She even managed a smile. The one she'd perfected over the past decade—the one that convinced people she was fine.

'I'm Ellis.'

'Hi.' She shook his outstretched hand. 'You're army too? Like Mattie?'

And Hayden. But for some reason she didn't add that bit.

'Yeah. I've done a couple of tours with Mattie over the years. You're a civilian doctor?'

'Nurse,' Bridget corrected, softening it with another smile.

Another mask to hide her regret at not being able to go to university to study medicine. Oh, she'd got the grades, but when she'd told her mother about her plans to move away from home, another breakdown had ensued, and Bridget had never broached the topic again.

'Oh.' The guy seemed surprised. 'Sorry, I'd just assumed… Anyway, Mattie holds you in high regard.'

This time, at least, the smile was more genuine.

'The feeling is mutual.'

'Yeah, Mattie's cool.' He grinned. 'But enough about our mutual friend. Can I interest you in a dance?'

'You want to dance?' It was too late to bite the words back. 'With me?'

First Hayden, now this guy. It had to be the dress. *Mattie's* dress. It wasn't *her*.

'I rather thought it might be a good plan, especially as we're in a nightclub. I don't know about you but us lot don't get that much chance for a night out like this.'

'No, Hayden was saying that earlier.' She bit her lip, wondering if lust was etched into every line on her face.

'You and Hayd have something…going on?'

'No.' She shook her head quickly. Maybe too quickly.

Bridget fought to smooth her face and offer a nonchalant shrug.

'I'm with the charity working near where his army unit will be working.'

'Operation Ironplate?'

'I guess.' As though she wasn't burning to learn anything new about Hayd. 'Like I said, I'm with the charity.'

Could the guy—Ellis—hear her heart hammering in her chest? She felt as though it was about to pound its way out, but he didn't seem to notice, so maybe she was okay.

'So you're not army barmy like us lot, then?'

He laughed. 'Well, I can tell you that Hayd is a great soldier and CO. You and your team are in good hands.'

'Right.' She nodded, forcing out the closest thing she could manage to a laugh.

'It's good to see Hayd back on operations.'

'He's been out?' Bridget's ears pricked up.

'Only recently. We've all done several back-to-back tours over the years and we're lucky we all got through them pretty much untouched—physically anyway. But Hayd was on a parachute jump about six months ago when some kid on his first jump passed out.'

Bridget sucked in a breath, not sure where Ellis's story was going.

'Oh, it's okay. Hayd had to cut his own parachute to dive and catch the kid in mid-air—not as common or as easy as the movies might lead you to believe—and he only had enough time to pull his emergency chute before the hit the ground, but he saved the kid.'

'Right…well, that's good,' she managed to choke out, telling herself that it was the drama of the story that had a wave of nausea sloshing around inside her. Nothing more.

'No, he's not likely to tell you either. But I've entrusted him with my life more times than I care to remember.'

Bridget nodded. And smiled again. Even though her teeth were gritted and her head felt as if it was jerking up and down. Knowing Hayden was such a true hero didn't really help her remember she was supposed to be staying away from him.

'So, how about that dance?'

She tensed instantly but tried to look as apologetic as she could.

'I…sorry… I don't actually…dance.'

'You look like you should,' Ellis tried again, but being encouraging rather than pushy. 'A couple of the others are out there on the floor, it doesn't have to be just the two of us.'

She relaxed a little and shook her head.

'Sorry.'

'Fine.' He looked disappointed but didn't push it as he headed for the dance floor, pausing to shoot her a final, open invitation. 'If you change your mind, you know where we are.'

Then he headed for the others, leaving Bridget wishing she'd had the courage to join him after all. And then Mattie was heading over, and Bridget relaxed even more.

'You okay, Bea?' her friend asked, before adding something else she didn't hear over the music.

'Sorry?'

Mattie leaned closer.

'I asked if Hayd has been looking after you?'

Heat rushed her again, making her cheeks feel hot.

'Yes,' Bridget managed. 'But you didn't really have to ask your brother to babysit me.'

'I *did* have to.' Mattie pulled an apologetic face. 'We were supposed to be working together at Jukrem camp—until I got called away for this new mission. I was really hoping to be able to show you the ropes out there.'

'It doesn't matter. I need to learn to be bolder anyway.' She forced a smile. 'Stronger.'

Like finally shedding the ties of her past and beginning to live the life she wanted to. Which probably included accepting an invitation to dance from a nice guy like Ellis and resisting this mad attraction to Mattie's brother.

'You're stronger than you realise, Bea,' Mattie suddenly said. 'You know what they say, fake it until you make it.'

'Yeah, well, I don't know how to fake it.'

'Sure you do.' Mattie laughed. 'Pretend you're that bushveld lizard you told me about. The one that pretends it's a boogie-oogie beetle, or something like that, to frighten away prey.'

'*Oogpister beetle*,' Bea corrected automatically, but she still laughed back just as she guessed her friend had intended her to do. 'I don't know what I'm more impressed with— your analogy or the fact you even remembered my story.'

'Both.' Mattie grinned. 'But either way my

brother will be there for any advice and support. Don't be afraid to use him.'

It certainly wasn't what Mattie had intended, but suddenly a thousand X-rated images of exactly what it might be like to *use* Hayden Brigham flooded Bridget's head.

And her body.

She flushed deeply and tried to shake her brain clear.

'Well, thanks.' The images were still there. In gloriously vivid colour. 'Anyway, enough about me, can I get you a drink to say congratulations?'

'Actually, it's traditional for me to buy you guys the drink since it's my promotion.' Mattie laughed, standing up and leaning over the table to address the members of the group who were left. 'Same again?'

And then she headed off, leaving Bridget to talk to the group and wish that she wasn't so very aware of where Hayden was, or what he was doing.

Or wondering whether maybe, just for once in her life, she might not do the sensible thing... but instead do the last thing in the world she should do.

And let her very first time with a man be with someone who would know exactly how to make her body come alive.

'Who's the guy? And why are you glaring daggers at him?'

He'd been avoiding her for the last couple of hours, but Bridget's voice cut unexpectedly across his thoughts. Hayden, moments from making his escape—having congratulated himself on thinking with his head and not other, less cerebral parts of his anatomy—turned quickly, arching his eyebrows at her.

He may have been avoiding her but that didn't mean he hadn't found himself sliding into group conversations when she was talking to others. Getting to know her whilst pretending he was keeping his distance.

He kept expecting this inconvenient and unexpected attraction to fizzle as he learned more about her. Telling himself that it was just the fact that she was a stranger—and a rather enigmatic one at that—that was causing him to react in such an uncharacteristic way.

Yet far from losing interest as the night had worn on, the more Hayden had seen and heard, the more attracted to her he'd become. Until in the end he'd had to tear himself away, telling himself it was time to head home.

But he hadn't gone, had he? He'd lingered around the booth where she'd come to join him, to talk to him. The music was louder now, and she was so damned close, and even though he knew it was the only way they could hear each other, he revelled in it all the same.

'So, do you know who he is?' Bridget reiterated, once it became clear that he'd forgotten to answer her.

Hayden tried to refocus his brain.

'His name is Kane. And I wasn't *glaring daggers* at him, as you so eloquently put it.'

'Well, I overheard you talking earlier. Mattie asked if you thought it was a bad idea for her to talk to this Kane guy, and you asked her if she needed you to tell her that,' Bridget observed softly. 'And now you don't look happy that your sister is still talking to him.'

He had to concede her point.

'Kane and Mattie knew each other a long time ago, when they were kids. They got together when she was sixteen, maybe seventeen,' he calculated. 'He hurt her.'

'That must have been about fourteen years ago.' Bridget whipped her head around to look at them. 'They look so…*involved* now.'

'Tell me about it,' Hayden grunted. 'Like the intervening years barely happened, and they're as close as they were back then.'

'Are they?'

'Are they what?' he asked through gritted teeth. 'Involved? I don't know but if they are then it's Mattie's life. Her choice.'

'But you don't like it?'

'Honestly… I don't know. She was devastated when Kane left her, and she's my kid sister. Part of me stills feel like I should look out for her. But she's also a grown woman, an army officer and doctor. She doesn't need me pulling big-brother rank on her.'

Bridget nodded, eyeing the pair of them again. 'I think it's kind of nice that you care, though.' She sounded almost wistful. 'I don't even have a brother.'

And, though he couldn't put his finger on it, Hayden couldn't help feeling that her casual comment revealed more than she'd intended it to. Even before she shook her head and pasted an overly bright smile onto her lips.

'Where were you going anyway?'

She was deflecting, and he couldn't have said why that caused something to scrape at him. To make him wish he knew what she was really thinking.

He pushed it aside.

'Actually, I was leaving.'

'Already?'

Something he fancied to be disappointment flashed in her eyes for a split second. Then it was gone, leaving him wondering it had been real or if he'd simply imagined it.

'We're leaving on operations in a couple of days. I might as well prep for it.'

'Tonight? No wonder you're such a good officer.'

Was she...flirting with him? If so, she was either doing it against her better judgement or she was simply not very good at it. Either way, he should take it as his cue to leave.

It was that or risk breaking every promise Mattie had elicited from him when she'd asked him to look after Bridget in her absence. Not that he was certain she needed, or even wanted, protecting, especially after she'd just handled Ellis's advances just fine.

Not that he'd been watching them, of course.

Not that he'd been *willing* her to turn the guy down.

'Yeah, tonight,' he confirmed. More for his benefit than for hers. 'The toasts have been done, everyone is breaking off into their own groups, it seems like a good time to leave.'

She frowned and Hayden realised he wanted, very much, to reach out and smooth her forehead flat again. With his mouth.

He forced himself to take a step back. Imperceptible to her, but hugely significant in his own head. Instead, she closed the gap, placing her hand on his forearm, making him *feel* her, all over.

'Take me with you.'

His chest pulled. Tightened. As did other parts of his anatomy.

'Say again?' he demanded, his voice somewhat gruff even to his own ears.

And then she flushed becomingly.

'I just… I just meant that… I only came to

celebrate Mattie's promotion.' The words tumbled out.

'You mean my sister bullied you into it?'

'I wouldn't say *bullied*.' She frowned again.

Hayden pulled his mouth into a thin line, as if that could temper these odd urges.

'The point is,' she continued, a little firmer this time, 'I came for Mattie, and now she seems... otherwise occupied. I don't really know anyone else.'

'Ellis seems to want to remedy that,' he managed evenly, although he felt anything but.

What was the matter with him? He sounded like a young boy in a school yard.

'No.' Bridget shook her head, blushing as prettily as ever. 'I think he's just being polite.'

She couldn't be serious.

'It's about more than just being polite, Birdie.' Her eyes met his then slid away. 'You must know that.'

The scarlet stain was creeping its way down her neck now. And lower. Hayden couldn't help wondering how far below that sexy neckline it extended, and he couldn't stop wishing he could find out.

'You really don't have any idea how attractive you are, do you?' he realised with surprise, as she startled, tried to shoot him a defiant glare, and then shrugged with embarrassment. 'Even without this.'

As if he couldn't help himself, he lifted his hand, making a small circling gesture, unsure whether he meant her screen siren body or the dress currently showcasing it so perfectly.

She took a step back, as if searching for the wall to lend her some support, taking refuge in the corner where the dark wall met the edge of the booths. Protected from the sight of the rest of group. Even most of the club.

But her eyes were on him and he was pretty sure she was flirting with him. Badly, but still. Just as he knew that she was as caught up as he was in this...*thing* between them. Somehow he made himself stay still and not step towards her. But that didn't mean he wasn't intrigued.

Sure, Mattie had asked him to look out for her friend because, in her words, Bridget was 'unworldly'. But he was beginning to suspect it was more than that.

He knew she was younger than Mattie by about five or six years, which would probably make her around twenty-six, maybe twenty-seven. So was it more that Bridget was inexperienced? If so, how much?

'You've had boyfriends before who've paid you compliments?' he mused, apparently idly.

'Hmm?' She pulled her eyebrows together and cocked her head, clearly not hearing him.

He took a step closer and tried not to feel like

a bull being pulled around by its nose ring. Then he repeated the question.

And there was no disguising the way the blood was beginning to thunder through his veins in a way that made absolutely no sense at all.

'Of course.' She jutted her chin out but refused to meet his eyes. In his experience, that was a tell-tale indicator that she was lying.

But about having had boyfriends? Or about them having paid her compliments?

'If not actual boyfriends,' he amended, leaning in closer like she was drawing him down, 'then those who might want to be?'

'Boyfriends?' she asked, and he could hear the shake in her voice before she jerked her chin higher. 'Or those who might flatter a girl to get into her underwear?'

There was something about the snippy way that she said it that made Hayden take notice. As though she was trying to appear more sophisticated and knowledgeable than she really was.

As if...

But, no, that couldn't be right. Still, he turned to face her fully, sliding his fingers to her chin and lifting it, just like he had before.

'And how many men have got into your underwear, Birdie?' He barely recognised his own voice. Or that primal, driving edginess slicing through him. 'A few? A couple? One?'

He could feel her breath, hot and fast on his

hand. See the way her chest was moving quickly, shuddery. Hayden couldn't help it, he wanted to stop himself, but he couldn't, she was too damn intoxicating. He dipped his head until his mouth was brushing her ear.

'None?'

She licked her lips, and it was all he could do not to catch it in his mouth.

'I don't really think that's any of your business,' she managed. 'Do you?'

And then, before he could say anything more, she lifted her trembling hands to his chest and spread her palms over him as though she meant to push him.

Only she didn't.

It was ridiculous that the action should burst inside him like a detonation. Before he could stop himself, Hayden stepped closer, pinning her to the wall, no longer able to pretend that he could resist her when his entire body was roaring at him to claim her as his own.

Shooting out his arm, Hayden rested his entire forearm on the wall by her head, not missing a single detail from her parted lips, from her rapidly rising and falling chest to the heat pouring off her—and into him.

And then he stopped noticing anything more as he dipped his head and fused his mouth to hers. Plundering her heat and raking his tongue against hers—ruthless and demanding—the way he'd wanted to do all night.

Something carnal and dark tore through him, and it was all he could do to keep it at bay. He'd never felt anything quite as *electric* as this before, and somewhere deep inside he knew that should have worried him a lot more than he was currently prepared to acknowledge.

And then Birdie surged against him, pressing her body to his as she angled her head to deepen their kiss, her hands reaching up very tentatively to cup his jaw, and he stopped thinking at all... he merely *experienced.*

He claimed her mouth over and over, learning its feel, its shape, its taste, sending him spiralling, half-delirious. And the fact that it was from a mere kiss only seemed to make it that much more insane.

His breath scythed between them, his body pushing him closer to edge than he could ever have imagined, and then Bridget raised her hands to loop them around his neck and pull him down to her with the most beautifully greedy sound he thought he'd ever heard, her body pressed against his.

Need shot through him. Lifting his hands, Hayden threaded them through the glossy, thick curtain of her hair. Subtle notes of coconut danced in his nostrils as he moved it, making him think of tropical beaches and hot sun, and Bridget's body naked beneath his.

He let himself explore some more. His hands moved down the long line of her spine, his mouth down the elegant line of her neck. Everything about this woman wound through him, making him hunger for more.

His hands learned the contours of her body, her backside, and then lower, abruptly coming into contact with the smooth, velvety skin of the back of her thigh.

White lights burst in his head. Her bare skin was so soft, and so damned hot. He should stop, he *ought* to stop, but when his fingers brushed her skin and she arched her body against his, he found he was lost.

Her mouth was still open under his, still inviting him in, still learning how to scrape her tongue against his as though dancing a sensual tango of their own. He pressed his body against hers even harder, needing to feel her heat against the hardest part of him.

Then, fanning his fingers out, he allowed them to slip slightly under the hem of her shimmering dress to that delicious crease where her legs met her peachy derrière. The greedy little sound she made was almost his undoing.

Hayden had never ached so badly in his life. He hadn't known it was possible to. He'd never felt as though he'd self-combust if he didn't get a taste of her, there and then. Yet with Bridget that was exactly how he felt. Before he knew what he was doing his hands spanned her thighs, his thumbs just creeping under the dress, the front of which—already short—had ridden up dangerously high, and stroked between her legs. Just once. But brushing right *there*, against a whisper of lace where she was searing hot, and so sinfully, perfectly wet for him.

Her moan rolled right through his body, and Hayden wasn't entirely sure how he didn't embarrass himself on the spot.

'You asked me how many men…before,' she managed, on a choppy little breath.

'Say again?' he muttered, his brain so fogged up he could barely think straight with wanting her.

'What if it was none?' she managed huskily, only the fact that his head was so close to hers allowing him to hear. 'Would that make a difference?'

Dear lord, she was a virgin, and she was offering herself up to him to be her first. He needed to walk away, but his legs refused to move.

He might have a reputation, but despoiler of virgins wasn't part of it. He preferred experienced partners who could enjoy a sexual encounter every bit as much as he did. Who knew what they wanted, and what they were prepared to give back—and said so.

Virgins had never been his thing. In fact, he'd always steered well clear of them in the past.

But this was different. *Bridget* was different. A fact that should set off more alarm bells than it was currently ringing. What was it about her that stirred something so intensely primal and feral within him? That made the idea that she could have lost her virginity to any number of suitors over the years but she'd saved herself to give such a precious gift to him?

He should be walking away.

All of a sudden, the sounds of the nightclub crashed back over him and he blinked as he came back to himself.

How had he lost all sense of where they were? Of who she was? Not just kissing in a public place but what he'd been doing to her had been practically indecent. In his whole life he'd never lost control like this.

He ought to be ashamed.

Instead, all he wanted was to pin her back in that corner and bury himself so deep inside her that neither of them would know where one of them ended and the other began.

It was insane.

'Take a moment to sort your dress out,' he told her through his teeth, turning his back to ensure no one had seen them.

Relieved to realise that no one had.

'I can't believe...' Bridget's voice sounded

shakily in his ear once she had readjusted her clothing. 'I don't make a habit—'

'Trust me, neither do I,' he grated back.

'I think… It isn't… Can we just forget it happened? Just leave?'

'I think that's the wisest course of action.' He nodded grimly.

Just as long as they weren't leaving together.

CHAPTER FOUR

'THIS IS TOMMY, nine years old. At approximately ten o'clock this morning Tommy began suffering an asthma attack. By the time we got there he was in respiratory arrest and the ventilating was deteriorating. There was vomit in the airway.'

Bridget listened to the heli-med doctor as he gave the MIST report—the Mechanism of Injury, the Illness pattern, the Signs or observations, and the Treatment given—to her team. It was her last case of this posting, before she was scheduled to fly out to her briefing for her new foreign aid mission in three days' time.

Less than a week from now she would be at Jukrem camp. And a few days after that Hayden and his regiment of Royal Engineers would be arriving.

Her pulse fluttered weakly, just as it had on each of the occasions she'd thought about him since that night at the club. And there had been far too many of those thoughts.

Cross with herself, she pulled her head back

into the present as the A and E doctor running the case began to address them.

'Let's get him stable so that we can get a scan and check for fluid in the airways,' the doctor running the shout concluded, and they each began to do their part. Putting on the monitors and administering the anaesthetic and the medications to try to regulate his stats.

Hour after hour. Interspersing it with other patients whenever there was a long enough lull. And then it was over. Bridget's shift was done and it was time for her to go home. Or rather to the cramped rented flat that passed for home.

No more cases of asthma, or diabetes, or emphysema—a few of the many things that had constituted the bread and butter of her UK work. Instead, she had to get her mind back into malaria, TB, measles and, almost always underlying it all, malnutrition.

And then there was the added complication of Hayden.

No matter how hard she tried to block it out, memories of the other night flooded her head, flushing her cheeks with heat—and her body with something even more molten. She shook her head viciously, as if that could somehow dislodge the inconvenient attraction, but it didn't work.

Had she really expected it to?

She couldn't ignore what had happened any more than she was going to be able to avoid seeing Hayden. The only solution was going to be to find a way to deal with it.

Lost in her thoughts, she was halfway out of the hospital grounds before she realised she'd walked past her bus stop. She could turn back around but it had stopped raining, and a perverse part of her welcomed the walk. As if it could somehow help her to clear her head.

Hayden was five miles into his eight-mile run when he saw her heading up the pavement towards him. The shock of it almost winded him, far more than the punishing pace he'd meted out to himself had managed.

He supposed he could have run past her as her head was bowed so low that she wouldn't have even noticed him until he was in line with her. Plus, he'd expected to have longer to wrap his head around how carried away he'd been the other night at the club. And he'd expected it to be in an army camp in the middle of the desert.

Still, much as he hated to admit it, he'd wanted to see her. Why else would he have chosen a running route that passed so close to the hospital in which she worked?

He slowed down. Stopped.

'Hello, Birdie.'

Her head snapped up in undisguised shock.

It was strange how seeing her again was a lot harder than Hayden had anticipated.

'Hayden.'

'Hayd,' he corrected. As though it mattered.

'Hayd,' she repeated carefully, like she was rolling it around her tongue.

And just like that he was back to the randy schoolboy of the other night, his mind full of all the other ways she could roll him around her tongue.

What the hell was it about her?

'What are you doing here?' she managed, breaking the silence. Looking altogether too cute and vulnerable for his peace of mind.

'Running.' He tried to suppress the smile that toyed with his mouth, not liking the way she got under his skin so easily.

'Running. Right.' She waved her hands at his shorts and tee in self-deprecation, and he found he didn't like that either. The way she always seemed to put herself down. 'Sorry. Obvious.'

And then, suddenly, a mask of indifference settled over her delicate features, and he found he liked that least of all.

'What about you?'

'I'm heading home.' She shrugged. 'I just finished my shift.'

'No car?'

Another shrug.

'I had an odd shift. Parking is always a nightmare.'

'Right.'

It was so stilted. So damned awkward. Like nothing he'd ever experienced before, which made him wonder how the next few months were going to go. They might not be working together per se, but their paths would certainly cross.

'Maybe we should…have a conversation,' he began.

Bridget, however, looked as though that was the least appealing activity she could think of. She shook her head vigorously.

'I don't think we should.'

'We're about to head out into an unfamiliar environment where we're going to be working in close enough proximity for three months. It's going to be difficult enough as it is, but if we don't resolve whatever…*this* is between us, it's going to be hell.'

'I think you made your feelings pretty clear when I basically…offered myself up to you and…and you rejected me.' She stumbled over the words in her haste to get them out, leaving Hayden to unravel them in her wake.

'Wait. I didn't reject you.'

She bit her lip.

'Of course you did. And I can't say I blame you. But I really don't want to talk about this with you. Especially in the middle of the pavement on a busy main road.'

'So go home, I'll head back to my hotel room to shower and change, and I'll pick you up within the hour. Maybe we could go for a drink.' Except what had happened the last time he'd been out with this woman, drinking? 'No, not a drink. But perhaps…grab a bite to eat.'

'To what? Talk about it some more?' She looked horrified. 'In the middle of a restaurant while trying to eat. No, thanks. I've had enough humiliation for one year. Admittedly, I probably brought it on myself.'

What the hell was she talking about?

'You didn't bring anything on yourself,' he countered, wondering why he was so fascinated by her.

Why even here, even now, his body was beginning to surge back into awareness.

'We need to resolve this, Birdie,' he said softly. 'Before we get into an environment where your inability to be around me causes problems for other people.'

'You're turning this on me?' she demanded incredulously, and that little spit of fire he remembered from the other night seemed to spark back into life.

'That depends. I'm willing to work this out. Are you?'

Then, as if things couldn't have gone his way any better, her stomach growled. Loudly. Hayden grinned.

'See, you *are* hungry after all.'

She spluttered for a moment then glowered at

him, but he didn't care. If anything, it gave him a bit of a kick low in his belly. Because at least it didn't mean that she was indifferent to him.

'Fine,' she huffed out at last. 'One hour.'

'I'll pick you up.'

'I'll meet you in town,' she countered. 'Where?'

He could argue the point, but did it really matter? At least she was meeting him.

'There's that Italian restaurant,' he suggested. 'Unless you have any objections.'

He refrained from goading her by adding *to that, too.* Still, she glared at him as though she could read it on his face.

'That's fine.' Her tone was clipped.

And then, before anything else was said, she turned away from him and stalked up the road, this time with her head held high in the air.

He watched her for far longer than he should have done, all the while telling himself there was no reason for his heart to beat so strongly, until finally he made himself turn and try to get his head back into his run.

And then he heard it. The roar of a large vehicle, the splash of water, and what was indisputably a shriek.

Spinning around, he saw a white van zooming past him. And Bridget, shouting furiously and soaked to the skin, next to a puddle the size of a small swimming pool. For half a moment he paused, waiting to see if the traffic lights ahead would turn red, ready to sprint down there and haul any one of the laughing men out of the van and show them exactly what happened to guys like them.

But the lights stayed mutinously on green, and the van sped off into the distance.

Turning back to Bridget and breaking into a run, he raced towards her and hauled her out of the way before any other vehicle could pile anything more on her obvious indignity.

'What did they do that for?' she cried, tears glistening in her eyes despite the water dripping from her hair. Her skin. Her clothes.

'Maybe they didn't see the puddle until it was too late.'

It wasn't true but he had no desire to upset her any further. He didn't want to examine that further, but then she lifted her head.

'Oh, they saw me,' she gritted out, the unexpected show of spirit drawing him in in spite of himself. 'They did it on purpose. Just for a laugh.'

'Be that as it may, the priority is to get you out of those clothes and dry. How far is your home?'

'Too far.' She shook her head, her voice quivering. A combination of anger and shock. 'The hospital is closer.'

But it was still a good mile back in the other direction. Hayden's mind spun, but there was nothing else for it.

'My hotel is closer. If we cut across the park, we can be back there within five minutes.'

'Your hotel?' She froze, blinking at him. 'Aren't you in barracks or whatever?'

'Usually,' he admitted. 'But every so often I like to get away from everyone else, and I fancied a few creature comforts.'

'That's exactly what I've heard Mattie say.'

'Not really a surprise, it was what our father used to do when he couldn't get home but couldn't face another night in the mess.'

'Right.' She nodded slowly, but her teeth were already beginning to chatter. 'Makes sense.'

Quickly he peeled her rucksack and wet coat off her, slinging the bag on his back and folding up the dripping material.

'Can you run? It'll keep up your core temperature and get us there quicker.'

'And what happens when we get there?'

She eyed him speculatively, and he tried not to point out that she was getting colder and colder the more she stayed immobile.

'If you're worried about being in the same room as me, I'll shower in the hotel's gym downstairs and you can have my bathroom. I wouldn't even enter the suite until you're happy, okay? I'll even get them to find you some dry clothes.'

He told himself he was being gentlemanly and ignored the growing suspicion that he simply didn't trust himself around this woman. Still, another moment passed before Bridget replied.

'No need. I have a change of clothes in my rucksack. They're in a dry bag so they should be fine.'

'Good.' He exhaled slightly. 'So if you're all objectioned out, maybe we could get going before you start making yourself ill?'

With a terse nod Bridget began moving. A little stiffly at first, but soon her legs seemed to loosen up and they were jogging across the wet grass. By the time they'd ducked around the railings and crossed the far road to his hotel, she seemed to have calmed down slightly, and he even heard her call out a cheerful greeting to a couple of elderly guests, who looked startled at her sodden appearance, suppressing her gurgle of laughter until they were in the lift.

And then she sobered again as they reached the door to his suite and he swiped the key card into the reader.

'I thought you weren't coming in?' she commented tensely, as he followed her inside.

Hayden held his hands up.

'Just getting a change of clothes then I'll be out of your way.' He efficiently opened the wardrobe and drawers to select fresh gear, before heading straight back to the door. 'Okay, I'm out of your hair. Take as long as you need.'

Closing the door behind him, he stood in the

corridor and wondered what it was *exactly* that
he thought he was doing.

Because far from clearing things up, as he told
himself he had intended, it seemed to Hayden
that all he'd succeeded in doing was making an
awkward situation all the more complicated.

CHAPTER FIVE

BRIDGET WATCHED THE hotel-room door close behind Hayden and then stood staring at the white panelling for an inordinately long time, trying to work out what it was that wallowed clumsily within her chest.

Why there was a part of her that seemed to be silently willing him to come back into the room. The *bed*room. And revisit with her everything they'd started in that nightclub.

Before he'd done the one thing that any true playboy surely shouldn't do…and listened to his conscience.

Which, if she was honest, didn't do much to reanimate her already moribund ego. It only fed into the fears that already lurked in her mind that she wasn't the kind of woman who was pretty enough, hot enough, sexy enough to appeal to a man like Hayden.

In short, she wasn't *good* enough.

Much as she'd stopped being *good enough* the night her father had been arrested. Overnight she'd gone from being a popular kid, an *it* kid, to being a pariah. No one had wanted to be seen even talking to her, let alone the girls wanting to hang out with her. And boys wouldn't have been caught dead dating her—although many of them had suggested quick sex in the back of a car, or an abandoned barn, or anywhere else they wouldn't be *seen* with her.

And she was proud that she'd never been so desperate that she'd allowed herself to fall for it.

Instead, she'd become an outcast, spending her teenage years living in the shadow of her father's disgrace and taking care of her ever more fragile mother, and her self-worth had never quite recovered. Holding onto her virginity had become less of a matter of pride and more a matter of embarrassment. How to explain to a potential lover that she was still a virgin in her twenties when everyone she knew had long since—willingly— lost that title.

Was that why she'd found herself so attracted to the idea of finally losing that burden with Hayden? A halfway playboy who would know what he was doing. A man who'd had enough partners that he wouldn't remember her and her inexperience.

Or was the truth that she hadn't been thinking at all when he'd kissed her the other night in the nightclub? Making her feel giddy and lightheaded. All her senses spinning so hard that she hadn't even been able to remember her own name, let alone the fact that she was letting him touch her so intimately in a dark corner of an otherwise public place.

As if he, too, had been carried away at that moment. Right up until the point where he had rejected her.

Oh, get over yourself! A sharp little voice sliced through her head. *So he doesn't want you.*

He was only here because he'd promised Mattie he would look after her. The best thing to do now was to shower and get ready, release him from this unnecessary duty as soon as he returned, and then get out of here.

Oh, Lord. Then again, weren't they supposed to be going for something to eat to discuss what had happened in that nightclub? To clear the air before the joint charity/army mission to Jukrem?

Forcing herself to start moving, Bridget made her way to the chair—deftly avoiding even looking at Hayden's bed—and let her rucksack drop from her shoulderbefore reaching for her change of clothes.

The shower was hot, and powerful. Better than the shower she had in her own apartment, and certainly better than the solar showers she'd be having over the next few months. Five minutes stretched into ten, and Bridget took her time washing her hair, and her body. Cleaning away not just the dirty rainwater from that grimy puddle but also the hateful memories, and her sense of inadequacy that Hayden Brigham had inadvertently unearthed. She scrubbed at it all until it was gone, leaving her feeling shiny, and fresh, and *whole* once more.

Then she let the water sluice over her as if she was under the most luxuriant waterfall in the world—and breathed.

By the time she had finished, blasting her hair quickly with the courtesy dryer before slipping into the soft pair of charcoal yoga pants and cropped tee that she had brought, Bridget felt new again. Happier.

More in control.

Until the soft knock at the door set her chest fluttering all over again.

Not so in control after all, she thought wryly.

Padding across the room, she drew in a deep breath and opened the door. Even before he entered the room, it felt to Bridget as though the walls were sliding in, making the space feel smaller and more cramped.

No. Not cramped. Full.

Hayden filled the space. Just as his very presence filled her chest with something she had never experienced before and couldn't identify even if she'd wanted to—though she didn't want to.

She didn't want to admit that, at twenty-six

years of age, she had never experienced anything quite like it before. She'd heard about it from friends, of course. Even read about it in the books they shared around the medical camps, thrilling in the happy-ever-after stories that offered them a glorious escape for as long as they stayed lost in the pages.

But she had never *experienced* it. Not even close. She hadn't even believed it really existed. And then she'd met Hayden, and he'd upended everything she'd held to be true.

'I'll just pack my things back up and I'll get out of your way,' she managed, trying not to scurry across the room.

'You don't have to feel awkward,' he told her softly.

She had to be imagining it to think there was a hint of triumph in his tone.

'Of course I feel awkward,' she retorted, her voice clipped but not quite enough to disguise the tremor in it.

She felt like a drowning woman struggling to break the surface and grab deep lungfuls of air.

'I let us…myself…get carried away in that club.' She made herself say the words, as ugly as they were. 'I did things I've never done before with anyone…and then you rejected me.'

Something flared in those Baltic blue pools, and it almost pulled her straight back under.

'No one else?'

'You think I make a habit of it?' She gritted her teeth.

Hayden didn't answer, he merely stood straighter and folded his arms across his chest, as though planting himself in place.

Why? Because he wasn't tempted...or because he was?

The questions chased one after another through her head—no matter how much she tried to squash them.

'Forget it,' she blurted out, reaching for her things, her hands shaking. 'I should go.'

'Wait.' It was a command. Low but unequivocal, and she found herself straightening slowly. Obeying. 'Let's get one thing straight. I did *not* reject you.'

'Please.' She tried to stay neutral but knew that self-disgust and shame had made her pull a face. 'You couldn't get out of there fast enough.'

He hesitated, and for a moment she thought he wasn't going to argue. That his silence was going to confirm her fears. She felt wrecked, and lost, and wholly confused.

And then his expression changed. Softened. As though he couldn't help himself.

'You're wrong, Birdie. I couldn't get out of there fast enough because I was about to lose my head. I *did* lose my head. I forgot where we were and nearly took you right there, against the wall in that club, you remember?'

She remembered. Oh, how she remembered.

How they hadn't been caught was a miracle and yet, even now, she wasn't sure she could have stopped if he hadn't.

'If we both wanted that…then why did we stop?'

'Apart from the fact that we were about to get it on in a public place, you mean?' His face twisted at the memory. 'Or that you're a virgin?'

'Is that what offends you most? That I'm a virgin?'

'Of course not. But you've been saving yourself all this time for a partner who will deserve you. I'm a player, Birdie, even my sister warned you off me. I can only end up hurting you.'

'You don't get it, do you? It isn't about deserving it or saving it. It isn't about getting hurt. It's about picking who and what I want.' She stopped, licked her lips, swallowed. 'And I want you.'

She wasn't even sure she recognised her own voice at that point, loaded as it was with something that felt dangerously like raw desire. *Need.*

'You don't want me.' He shook his head, but his voice was too thick. 'Trust me, you don't know me.'

'I want you. One night, that's all.'

'You're not the kind of girl who does *one* nights.'

'I might be, I just haven't tried it yet.'

'You're not.' His voice sounded strangled, and she liked it that she was getting to him. 'You're the kind of girl who holds out for more. Who deserves more.'

'You don't know as much as you think.'

'I know I'm not a good man, Birdie,' he warned her.

But his voice rumbled deliciously, and something shifted through those clear blue pools, sliding inside her and working its way down her body.

'Maybe I don't want a good man,' she bit back. 'Maybe a bad man is exactly what I need.'

'Birdie…'

There was no denying the answering note in his voice. As greedy and demanding as the call roaring through her entire body. And when she allowed her hungry gaze to roam his body, she realised the tell-tale shadow—right where he was hardest—gave away all the things he was trying to keep from her.

Hayden Brigham *did* want her. *Badly.* It was the headiest feeling she'd ever known. Bridget felt her hands begin to shake, her entire body start to tremble. But not with fear or uncertainty, but anticipation.

Either she had to be bold now or she had to live with regret for the rest of her life. It really was now or never.

Sliding her hands down to the waistband of her

yoga pants, she hooked her thumbs inside and then pushed them down in one smooth movement until they were lying in a soft puddle at her bare feet. She stepped out of them.

'What are you doing?' It was a warning, but it was hoarse and lacked any real punch.

Bridget chose to ignore it. Instead, she took the hem of her tee and pulled it over her head, leaving it to fall on top of her trousers. And then she was standing there wearing only her prettiest, wispiest thong.

And an expression that dared him to make the next move.

'Birdie,' he muttered, but he didn't add anything else. And he didn't move.

For a moment she almost faltered, but she could hardly stop now. Not when she'd already stripped. At least Hayden looked tormented rather than, say...*disgusted*.

Slowly, very slowly, she took first one step towards him. Then another. And Hayden shook his head weakly but he didn't speak.

'Cat got your tongue?' she asked sweetly, pretending that her heart wasn't clattering noisily behind her ribcage.

'You'd better be sure this is what you want, Birdie,' he growled at last. 'Because if you come much closer, I can't guarantee my actions.'

'How much closer?' She barely recognised

that husky, needy voice as her own. 'This much closer?'

She took another step.

'This much?'

Reaching out, she slid one finger down the front of his trousers, to the part of him that fascinated her most, revelling as the sound seemed to hiss out of Hayden.

He was hard. So hard she felt a resounding throb between her legs.

She was the one who had got him that way.

'Birdie.' He circled her wrist with his fingers. Not painfully but firmly. 'All these years you've waited. To give that gift to me…be certain that it's what you want.'

'I'm standing here in front of you, for all intents and purposes naked,' she choked out. 'How much more certain can I be, Hayd?'

She had no idea if it was the words or saying his name, but he gave in to her with a groan, snaking his hand around her neck and hauling her to him, crushing his mouth to hers and setting her alight like he'd dropped a match into a tank of petrol.

Bridget went up in flames.

He tasted her, sampled her, possessed her. And all she could do was cling to him and let him sweep her along on the ride, opening her mouth to him and feeling his tongue raking against hers just as it had the other night.

Just as she'd dreamt about every night since.

He angled his head, deepening the kiss and taking her mouth over and over again. Almost as if he'd forgotten that she was practically naked in his arms.

She didn't know whether to think that was a good thing or a bad thing. Then again, she didn't know that she could think very much at all, especially when his mouth slid so slickly across hers, his teeth stopping every now and then to draw one of her lips between his.

And then, suddenly, he let his hands drop. Skimming down her body, tracing her shape, testing her, as if trying to memorise every curve and every contour. Her skin leapt under his touch, sizzling and scorching, making her want to press her body as close to his as she possibly could. It still wasn't enough.

Pulling her arms around, Bridget sought out his shirt, fumbling with the hem until he stilled her, and she could feel his lips curving against hers.

'There's no rush.'

'I want to feel you,' she managed. 'Against me.'

'I am against you.'

They both knew he was teasing her. Testing her.

'Naked,' she clarified boldly.

'Ah.' Taking the T-shirt in his hands, he swept

it over his head and launched it somewhere across the room. 'Why didn't you just say so?'

But Bridget didn't answer. She couldn't. All she wanted to do was feast her eyes on Hayden's chest with its defined muscles and never-ending ridges. Like nothing she'd ever seen before.

Slowly, almost reverently, she ran her hands over him. Fingertips first then palms. Up and round his chest, his shoulders, those arms. If she'd had the courage, she could have followed it up using her mouth, but she still wasn't sure enough of herself. Or of her effect on Hayden.

Though that was becoming clearer.

And then, before she could think what else to do, he dipped his head down to her neck and planted a host of devastating kisses in the sensitive hollow between her neck and her shoulder.

Bridget was helpless to resist. Letting her head fall back, she arched against him, and as she did so her nipples, already tight and aching, brushed against the fine hairs on his chest, making her gasp aloud. Her hands were pressed against his shoulder blades, her fingers biting into his skin.

'Hayd…' she muttered, wanting more. *Needing* more.

As if he could read her mind, he dropped his head lower, trailing kisses down over the swell of her chest and straight to one aching, straining nipple. And he sucked it straight into his mouth.

Everything began to spin. She felt desperate

and wild, feverish all over. All she could do was try to hold onto the edge of her sanity as she finally began to regain some kind of footing.

And then he scooped her up and carried her across the room to the big bed, laying her down until she was sprawled in front of him for his eyes to feast on, before he groaned and removed the rest of his clothing with shocking efficiency.

Lord, how beautiful he was. And honed. And male.

Very, *very* male.

Almost mesmerised, she used her elbows to push herself into a sitting position, her hands reaching for him as if on autopilot.

'No.' The low guttural sound shuddered through her, sinful and perfect.

And then, before she could rationalise anything, he gently pushed her back on to the bed, lifted one leg, and began to kiss his way up it.

Bridget watched, mesmerised, as he made his way from the inside of one ankle up to the inside of the knee, indulging, meandering, taking his time. She watched, even more hypnotised, as Hayden progressed from her knee up the inside of her thigh, his kisses growing hotter and more laden with promise as he advanced up the ever more sensitive flesh. Until he was…*there*.

Right there.

And her body was quivering wildly in anticipation of what was about to happen, even as her brain was struggling to take it all in.

She watched, bewitched, as he lifted his eyes to meet hers, that naughty curve of his mouth still working its way up the last inch of inner thigh.

'Hayden,' she muttered, only half understanding.

His grin broadened, even as those pools of blue darkened, and suddenly he lowered his head between her legs.

Bridget cried out. Loudly. She heard herself through the fog but was helpless to stop. She'd heard about it, read about it, even had female friends go into detail about it, but nothing could possibly have prepared her for how the pure sensation of it felt.

Or perhaps how it felt when Hayden did it. His mouth on her sex, his tongue licking its way into her core, went way beyond all that she'd ever imagined it would be. It felt like rocketing up through the troposphere, the stratosphere, to the very exosphere. It felt like she never wanted it to stop. Or to come back down again.

She wanted more yet she didn't know if she could stand it. Gripping his shoulders, Bridget writhed and moaned, barely recognising her own voice, and the low growls of approval that Hayd made—the sounds that rumbled their way from the back of his throat and into her very body—

only turned her on all the more. Wantonly bucking her hips up to meet his mouth, shamelessly begging him for more.

'Please, Hayd.'

'Please?'

'Please?'

And the worst—or best—of it was that she didn't even know what she was begging him for. Not until he closed his lips around her and sucked. Hard. One finger slid easily inside her and sent her soaring into space all over again as everything turned into a brilliant, white light. She was hurtling into nothing, and she didn't care. And then, suddenly, he twisted his hand and slid another finger inside her, and Bridget heard herself shatter with a glorious scream, calling out his name as though it had always been meant to be this way.

She had no idea how long she was out of herself, but by the time she came back down to earth, Hayden was lying next to her, a dark, unfathomable expression on his hewn features. Who knew what it was about it? But if she'd been able to capture that look and put it in a bottle, Bridget suspected she'd be able to hold onto this incredible, intense sensation forever.

'That was…' she began hesitantly.

'Only the start,' he assured her with a grin. 'Are you ready for more?'

Was she? She didn't know if she could handle more. But she certainly wasn't about to say no.

Before she could answer, however, Hayden was leaning over to the drawer, reaching for a foil packet—and part of her considered that she ought to be ashamed that the thought of protection hadn't even entered her head, she'd been so caught up in the moment—and deftly dealt with it.

Then he was sliding his sublimely solid body back over hers, gathering her up in his arms whilst her legs opened up to him as if by instinct, and all other thoughts fled from her mind.

He nudged against her. Velvet and steel where she was hot and so very wet. She could feel herself blush again, shifting slightly in her uncertainty, but then he let out a low, carnal groan, and Bridget wondered if she perhaps had a little more power than she'd realised.

Lifting her smaller hands to his well-defined shoulders, she shifted again, drawing him inside her, deeper than he'd intended to go.

A slow sound hissed out of Hayden's mouth as he gritted his teeth, clearly trying to regain some control as he drew back out of her, and Bridget found it inordinately satisfying that she'd caught him off guard, wresting some of his power from him.

She waited until she felt him flex again and

then carefully, experimentally, she shifted once more and drew him deeper inside.

'Careful, *Birdie*,' he growled deeply, and the sound thrilled her ears. 'If you push us any faster, I can't promise you I'll be able to hold back.'

'And here was I thinking you were some kind of expert playboy,' she teased, not knowing from where this sudden show of courage was coming.

'I was,' he gritted out again. 'Until you.'

Then, not allowing her the chance to argue, he reached down between them and started playing with her. Long strokes, fast swirls, anything that made her head drop back and her breath come in short, choppy bursts all over again.

The man was far too devilish for his own good.

'I want you,' she whispered, her hands gliding down his back and her fingernails gently grazing as they moved.

He shivered against her, sliding in deeper, and she gasped.

'You're not helping.' His voice sounded half-strangled and Bridget found that she loved that most of all.

'I'm not trying to help,' she whispered back. 'I'm trying to make you come apart the way you just did for me.'

'This time we'll do it together.'

She lowered her eyes, not wanting to meet his. Not liking the idea of reminding him how inexperienced she was.

'I don't think I can.'

'Oh, Birdie…' He sounded amused even through his pained tone. 'I'm going to prove to you how many times you can.'

As she opened her mouth to respond, he started moving, slowly at first but still every sound was snatched away from her.

There was *pain*…only not. It was there for a brief moment and then it wasn't. Leaving instead a dull sensation. She might have to say a kind of…stretching. But along with it the shocking realisation that Hayden was sliding inside her.

His long, thick length was going all the way inside her, and her brain was thrilling at the notion, even as her body was making its objections known.

'Relax,' he murmured. 'I promise I'll be gentle.'

'It…pulls.'

'So give it a moment.' He dropped his forehead to connect softly with hers, as though he was having to control himself more than she'd realised.

Bridget didn't know what it was about that fact that made her want to shift her hips—but she did it. And then, as his eyes held hers, the expression in them darkening with desire, she tried it again. And again.

'Better?' he demanded hoarsely.

She grinned.

'I'd say so.'

'Fine,' he announced grimly, beginning to move. And only then did Bridget realise her mistake.

Awareness flooded her. And need. As he set a leisurely pace, she felt herself melt around him. Her body cried out for him and her knees began to rise up to draw him deeper. Instinctively, her hands moved down to his backside to encourage him further.

'I don't know what you're doing to me,' he gritted out, 'but I swear you're killing me, Birdie.'

'I don't know what I'm doing either,' admitted Bridget. 'I only know I want you. Inside me. Deeper.'

If this was sex, she had no idea what it must be like to be in love.

'I'm trying to go gently,' he managed.

She nodded, her words little more than whispered.

'I know. But I don't think I want you to be gentle with me.'

As if to prove her point, she lifted her legs entirely and wrapped them around his hips, plunging him deeper inside her. He groaned, a visceral, carnal sound, and then he began moving faster. And each time Bridget lifted her hips to meet him, he plunged into her deeper and faster, as though he was no longer in control, until all she could hear was their ragged breathing. Proof that she wasn't the only one so close to the edge.

Dipping his head, Hayden found the juncture of her neck and shoulder again, making her arch her back and thrust her breasts against his chest, her nipples raking across his smattering of hairs and driving her wild.

With every stroke she clung to him harder, opened to him more. Deeper, and faster, and stronger. And for a moment everything hung around her, captured in a perfect snapshot in time.

But then she was flying again, rushing towards a brilliant light, unable to stop herself. Only this time when she fractured, and splintered, and finally fell, all the while screaming Hayden's name, he followed her, calling out her name, too.

It was pitch black when Hayden woke, with her still in his arms. The subtle coconut scent of her luxurious hair infiltrated his nostrils, making him want to inhale deeply. To breathe in the essence of *her*.

They'd made love—*had sex*, he corrected himself swiftly—twice more since that first time. Once in the shower and once back in bed. And even now his body started to harden, aching to take her again. And again.

He couldn't quite shake the odd sensation that

moved through him. As if this woman was different from any other that he'd known. As if he was never going to quite get enough of her.

The next instant he shoved it aside.

Ridiculous.

Still, he didn't want to move. He didn't want to break contact with her. But, perhaps sensing his wakened state, Bridget stirred in his arms, stretching elegantly before opening her eyes.

And blinked at him.

He might not be able to explain it but there was no stopping the grin that spread across his face. He found that he was captivated by her. And he had to tell himself, several times, that he didn't like that fact.

It wasn't until she shifted in his arms, her expression shutting down, that he realised he'd started to frown.

'Should I...go?' she asked hesitantly.

'No, don't.'

He hadn't meant to say it. In fact, he'd been telling himself that if she left it was probably for the best. As if to compound things, he opened his mouth again, his voice just as rough and abrasive.

'Stay.'

'Stay?' she breathed, clutching the sheet in her delicate hands and pulling it up to cover her breasts.

A fact that his brain—and his body—were already lamenting.

'Stay,' he repeated, reaching over to pull her back down onto the bed. And onto him. 'A little longer.'

'With you?'

He heard his own laugh, like a roll of thunder, and wondered how it sounded like nothing he'd ever heard before. Yet he laughed. Not infrequently either. But never like this, with such pleasure.

'Definitely with me,' he growled, before settling her astride him.

Her entire, sublime fifties pin-up body on show for him. Her glossy, black hair cascading over her shoulders, down her back, sneaking over one breast.

He reached out and brushed it away, his body tensing even more as she exhaled and shivered on him when he brushed one already taut nipple.

'Is this just muddying things that we've complicated enough?' she asked, but he couldn't help but notice that she said it with more than a little reluctance.

They both knew what they were doing was insane, but neither of them could bring themselves to stop.

'In less than a week we'll be in a foreign country,' he noted. 'You'll be looking after people, and I'll be looking after your clinic, making sure there is adequate drainage, fresh water, power.'

'I know that.' She pursed her lips. 'So how

does that help what we're doing here? Now? Surely it's…inappropriate.'

'It's a complication perhaps. Though not inappropriate. But in any case it means there's a clear line between the two things. Here, and there.'

And he was damned well going to ignore the niggling doubt that it wouldn't be that easy. That drawing that line, and sticking to it, were very different things. Especially, it seemed, where his libido and Bridget Gardiner were concerned.

'A line,' she repeated carefully. 'Like *What happens in Vegas stays in Vegas*?'

'Exactly,' he declared, fighting the almost overwhelming urge to move his hands to her hips.

She eyed him dubiously.

'And that works? It's that easy?'

'Why not?' he answered, shoving aside the simple truth that he'd never had to worry about it before because he'd never been tempted to cross his own self-imposed lines before.

Or the fact that, with Bridget, he hadn't merely crossed them as much as skidded over them, blotting them out altogether.

'Or we can stop,' he forced himself to say, even though he knew that stopping himself from touching this particular woman might well kill him.

Colour flushed her cheeks and she dropped

her eyes to his chest, following the trail as her hands moved over the ridges they found.

'I don't think I *could* stop,' she whispered.

'Then we won't,' he ground out, need overtaking him once more.

And he used his hands to guide her onto him, wanting to take his time but driven on by the sight of her body moving on him, and as she dropped her head back, pushing herself down onto him, he thrust his way home as though it had always been this way.

CHAPTER SIX

THE FLAP TO the ICU room was snapped back and one of her colleagues burst through, carrying a young child in her arms, malnourished and pale. Bridget snapped her head up from task of finishing up loose ends at the end of her shift and hurried over.

'He was brought into the paediatric outpatient feeding centre. But he isn't breathing, and his pulse is slow,' Lisa announced, laying the child on the bed.

Swivelling around, Bridget grabbed the bag mask ventilator and connected it to the oxygen and began prepping the adrenalin as another nurse called the time, and Lisa began chest compressions.

Briefly it crossed Bridget's mind that the weight loss could be a symptom of malaria, TB, measles or any number of other issues out here on the African continent, but until they got him breathing and stable, there was no way they could even begin to diagnose. She wasn't sure how long they worked for, sweat pouring off them in the forty-degree heat, but eventually the boy was breathing on his own again, albeit wearing an oxygen mask, his pulse returning to normal.

She sent out a silent thanks that it was a better outcome than the previous day when they'd worked for thirty minutes, only for the little girl to have to be declared dead. This time, at least, it was a happier end to what had been a long, draining shift.

'It's quiet this evening,' she observed, looking around the room.

'There were no new admissions so the clinic was shut down early,' Lisa agreed. 'Skeleton crew on for tonight—some last-minute plan, I heard. Anyway, your shift is done. Go. Relax. I'll see you tomorrow.'

'Okay, 'night, then.' Bridget hesitated, looking around one more time to check there was no work still to do.

'Go,' Lisa ordered with a laugh, making her slink sheepishly to the door.

'Yes, yes, I know. I'm going.'

As Bridget walked out of the tent, she stood in the heat and turned her face up to the sun for a few moments. Breathing in the hot, fresh air, and trying to remember if she'd ever felt so tired. She'd only been in the medical camp for four days, yet it felt like a lifetime. It was terrifying, exhausting, and—when they managed to save a life—the most satisfying feeling in the world.

Not that she hadn't felt that way back home, but it was always different out here where even the most basic medical supplies weren't freely available to these people.

Her first day in—arriving by plane and flying over miles and miles of dry arid, pretty much barren land—she'd been brought to the clinic, such as it was, to witness a little boy of about six, comatose and seizing.

The probable diagnosis had been meningitis, which back home would have meant the young child would have been sedated and ventilated, and he would have been monitored. He would have a feeding tube and a catheter, whilst a central line would have been put in, and a neuro monitor would have been attached to catch low-grade seizure activity. But out here none of that was available.

Even now, Bridget could remember her very first case on her very first mission, many years ago. A small child very similar to this little boy. She recalled listening as her mentor had explained to her that she would simply have to monitor regularly herself by lifting the eyelid and looking for faint flickering, or even just test the arm for rigidity, to determine whether there was seizure activity. Then it was a matter of using the vitals to determine fluid boluses or diazepam.

'How will I know how much to use?' Bridget could still remember such a feeling of helplessness as she'd asked the question.

And she could still picture her mentor's half smile, half grimace.

'Look at the vitals.' The woman had shrugged. 'Too little and the seizures will continue. Too much and you'll cause respiratory depression. We do the best we can out here.'

She'd returned to her accommodation feeling more frightened than ever. Yet, only a few days in, and Bridget had already begun to find her sea legs.

Now, several missions and years later it felt horribly *normal*.

She saw measles, malaria and meningitis on a daily basis, and she had already delivered more babies in four days than she would probably have delivered in four months back home. But she hadn't grown used to the deaths yet. She hoped she never would.

The main problem with where they were was that it was so far into the bush that there was no town, no market, certainly no hospital. Which meant that people simply weren't used to having medical help around—not unless they walked for two days or more to the nearest big town with its understaffed, under-equipped hospital—and so they didn't come into the charity's small clinic until it was too late for Bridget or her colleagues to be able to really help.

As she rounded the corner to the small *tukul* she shared with another nurse, Bridget stopped short when she saw her roommate painting her toenails a glorious shiny red.

'Bad day?'

'Thankfully not.' Sara smiled, barely looking up from her task. 'I just fancied feeling a little more…feminine. At least, as much as one can, dressed in combat trousers, a tee and dusty sandals all day long.'

She shifted around on the corner of her hammock to allow Bridget to enter the one-roomed mud hut, containing the two beds—each complete with mosquito net—and something that passed for a chest of drawer per person.

Ultimately, the plan was to use local expertise to build more *tukuls* so that each member of staff would have a small haven that they could call their own. But at the moment a broken roof in what would ultimately become the main accommodation area in one of the abandoned village's old buildings meant the rooms there were unusable, and many of them were having to share.

'Want to borrow it?' Sara waved her bottle of shiny red nail polish in the air. 'We can call it our version of party gear.'

Bridget frowned.

'There's a celebration?'

'Close enough.' Sara laughed. 'The army unit came in this afternoon, and we're throwing them a bit of a welcome party as we're going to be working together so closely for the next few months. See if we can't break the ice a little to make the *getting to know each other* process that little bit smoother.'

Bridget pitched forward, grateful that her hammock was there to catch her fall, not that Sara seemed to notice.

So *that* was why the clinic had been shut down early and there was only a skeleton crew on. Usually, the charity tried to have roommates on alternating shifts, so that one would be working when the other had down time, thereby allowing each of them to get some valuable alone time in the *tukul*. But tonight the charity was hosting a sort of party for the army camp, an effort to get to know each other given how they were both working in the area. So she and Sara both had down time for the evening, unless an emergency came in.

It had been almost a week since she'd left Hayd's bed. But it had taken her a lot longer to get him out of her head.

Her mind had been full of memories of him the entire flight to the charity's headquarters, all through the briefings and seminars, and the whole duration of the flight out here. Even during the short plane ride from the capital city to the tiny airstrip closest to the charity's new camp in Jukrem—which she would normally have spent drinking in the stunning views of lush vegetation after the rains—had been filled with X-rated images of Hayden Brigham.

So much so that it had been a relief to be ushered into the clinic almost the moment her four-by-four had pulled into the camp, so that the outgoing nurse could begin her handover. The bedlam of the over-subscribed outreach clinic proved to be just the distraction that Bridget had needed. And today she'd almost—*almost*—forgotten that she was meant to be forgetting about him.

But now he was here. His regiment of Royal Engineers had finally arrived, and she was going to have to deal with him on a daily basis. And suddenly she wasn't so sure she could face him without remembering everything he'd done to her with his mouth, his fingers and more.

She shivered deliciously then instantly tried to quash it.

What had happened that night was over. Done. It wouldn't be happening again, and the sooner she remembered that, the better for everyone. She wasn't out here to further anything with Hayd, or anyone else for that matter, she was out here because she had a job to do. A job she'd performed perfectly on many previous occasions.

'Did you want to borrow it?' Sara's voice crashed in on Bridget, and she looked up to see her roommate screwing the top closed and holding it out into the gap between the beds.

Bridget hesitated. She'd been through enough camps to have seen doctors do similar things over the years. Sometimes nail polish, sometimes mascara. One had even had pretty rhinestone Alice bands. And she'd been tempted.

It was hard to feel feminine out here sometimes with all the muck, and dust, and disease.

But in the end she'd never wanted to enough, so surely there was no need to let herself get distracted now? Just because Hayden Brigham was finally at camp?

He meant nothing to her, she reminded herself. They'd drawn a clear line between the UK and out here, and out here he meant nothing to her. She wasn't buying it.

Indeed, even in the UK he was just the man who had finally helped her to offload her inconvenient label of being a *virgin.* Nothing more.

And certainly not the reason why she reached out and took the gloriously red bottle from her roommate, murmuring her gratitude and wondering what...anybody else might make of it.

Hayden held the neck of his beer bottle in his fingers and leaned on the pillar, only half tuned in to the conversation going on beside him between his second-in-command and the charity's mission leader as he watched the rest of the reception play out in front of him. Pretending he wasn't looking out for *her*. The woman who had haunted his thoughts for the better part of the past week.

No matter what he'd said, that night in his hotel suite, about drawing a line between what had happened between them in the UK and how they would be out here in a professional capacity, he'd found that his thoughts had wandered back to Bridget too many times to count over the last few days.

How many times had he woken up, his body hard and ready after worryingly vivid dreams of her? As though nothing would ever sate him the way that this woman had done.

He was, therefore, intensely grateful that his army camp was separate from the charity's medical compound. Whilst they were making use of the buildings in an abandoned village while the army effected some of the repairs for them, his Royal Engineers, along with a logistics unit and some other support troops, were no more than a couple of hundred metres away on the opposite side of a dried-up riverbed.

It wasn't much of a divide in terms of terrain, but it was the psychological divide that he needed. The reassurance that he could focus on his task in hand. The confidence that he wasn't going to run into Bridget on a daily basis.

Because whatever else that night back in his hotel room had done, it had convinced him that one night with her wasn't nearly enough. It hadn't sated this smouldering need inside him—it had stoked it up.

He wasn't entirely convinced that anything would douse it, bar taking her to his bed. Again, and again. And it didn't matter how many times he told himself that he didn't mix work and pleasure. Or that virgins weren't his thing. Or even that, as much as his parents had made their relationship work, he'd still seen how it had affected his mother, being married to a military man who had been away more than he'd been home. He'd promised himself long ago that he would never put any woman through the same.

Now he was fighting the nonsensical notion that he'd only found it so easy to stick to that promise because he'd never found the right woman before.

'What do you think, Hayd?'

The question crashed through his thoughts. Pasting a polite expression over his features, he turned to his companions.

'Say again?'

'I was explaining to Mandy that the surveys we've been conducting all week have primarily been recces to determine whether the intel sent to us back in the UK matches the actual set-up on the ground before we can decide which pieces of infrastructure should be our priority.'

'Yes, I completely understand.' Mandy, the charity's mission coordinator, bobbed her head enthusiastically. 'I just wanted to make sure you understood that the ground conditions you're seeing now are vastly different from the conditions we encountered when we first arrived here a couple of months ago.'

'In the wet season?' Hayden forced himself to focus. To stop looking out for a woman whose presence should have no impact on him whatsoever.

'Right,' Mandy agreed. 'This part of the country gets muddy, swampy. We'd intended to be in a month earlier, but we had to postpone it because even the airstrip had been close to being reclaimed by the mud. The dry riverbed you see out there now was close to overflowing. The locals build roads each year but each year they get washed away when the floods come.'

'So your concern is that we'll focus on what makes sense now, without appreciating the terrain could look very different in six months? Or eight?' Hayden confirmed.

'Yes. I'm just conscious that the army is only here as a bit of a Section 106.'

'I'm sorry?'

She shot him a look that was only half-apologetic, but he was beginning to like her anyway. She was direct and down to earth, and he'd always found that much easier to work with than trying to guess what someone *wasn't* saying.

'You know…a bit of *quid pro quo.* You're getting a training area in this region on the basis that you put in a little infrastructure. And I'm very grateful for that, believe me. But I've been working out here for a long time, mostly in the main hospital a few hours' drive away. It matters to me—to this charity—that we make the most of you whilst you're here. Put in the base work that will most benefit the villages here on a long-term basis.'

'Which is why I'm more than happy to take on board any and all advice you give us,' he told her sincerely. 'Aside from the fact that I *want* to do as much as possible to help the people of this region, it's also in the army's interests to do so. So if you want to accompany me on a recce tomorrow, and perhaps let me run you through where I'm up to so far, I'd be happy to get your feedback?'

'Great.' Mandy gave a pleased smile. 'I'd really appreciate that. I think it's going to be a pleasure to work alongside you, even if not on a regular basis. If you'll excuse me, I should make a social round of my people. I see a few of the new volunteers and I want to introduce them so that handovers are easier.'

'Of course,' Hayden agreed, as his second-in-command asked to join her.

Then, stepping back, Hayden watched as they left.

'Welcome to Jukrem, Hayd.'

He knew he shouldn't care, and yet he turned around almost eagerly.

'I was beginning to think you were on duty tonight.'

'I was…painting my toenails.'

He could tell she wished she could bite back the words the instant they fell from her lips. Still, he couldn't help his eyes from dropping down to the dusty, unflattering sandals that the charity workers tended to wear around here. Although they probably beat the hot desert boots his guys had to wear in such heat.

Glossy, bright red nails stared back at him, and he felt the corners of his mouth tug.

'Very dainty.'

'You're laughing at me,' she accused.

'Not at all,' Hayden corrected. 'I'm laughing *with* you. There's a difference.'

She grunted slightly but didn't answer immediately.

'Looks nice,' he added.

'I know you might think it sounds silly,' she informed him airily, 'but it's amazing how a hint of something like this can restore some degree of femininity, especially in a place like this.'

'Right,' he gritted out.

The last thing he needed was to be reminded of how gloriously feminine Bridget was. Like he wasn't barely keeping a grip of himself as it was.

Her expression changed and she looked almost disappointed. As if he had somehow let her down.

It should concern him how much that got to him.

'I've been here less than a week, but I know that as the months go by something like seeing my toenails a pretty colour could lift my mood. We go around all day in combat trousers and neck-choking Ts, covered in dust, or mud, or worse—blood. A bit of nail polish helps you to feel like you're still a woman underneath it all.'

'I wasn't judging,' he heard himself say.

'Well…good,' but she still didn't look convinced, and before he realised it he was speaking again, a soft smile pulling at his mouth.

She had softened him.

'Have you ever read the diary of Lieutenant Colonel Mervin Willett Gonin?'

'I don't know who that is…' She frowned.

'He commanded a field ambulance brigade in Belsen concentration camp back in 1945.'

'Oh.'

'In his diary, he recalls how he and his men were crying out for supplies to help with diphtheria, dysentery, severe malnutrition. Their conditions were inhuman. There was so much equipment his brigade needed but couldn't get hold of. Then the British Red Cross arrived, and shortly afterwards a crate of lipstick turned up.'

She watched him closely, her attention piqued. Something shifted through him.

'It wasn't what his men wanted at all, it wasn't going to help heal those people, yet it ended up being an act of genius. After years of being treated worse than animals, nothing more than the number tattooed on their arm, the women were suddenly given something to restore their humanity. A humble red lipstick. It made them feel like they were people again, like they were alive. So, yes, Birdie, I understand how the simple act of painting your nails could be uplifting.'

For a moment he could see her pondering and he wished he knew what was going on in her head.

'I wish lipstick and nail varnish could help everyone.' She exhaled deeply at last. Relaxing a little and letting her guard down again. 'I had a patient this morning, a young girl barely older than fifteen who had been caught with a spear blade. The local men had been out hunting and she'd been in the wrong place at the wrong time.'

He nodded in empathy, though a part of him lamented the fact that she'd had to slip back into her old routine of dodging the personal and sticking with the work-related in order to talk to him.

'The injury was severe, and they'd treated her the best they could, using what medicines they had available to them, but she needed surgery. She was feverish, hallucinating and there were clear signs of sepsis, and we don't have the surgical facilities here in Jukrem, so we were lucky we happened to have a surgeon visiting from the main hospital for a couple of days, who was able to carry out a full hysterectomy and save her life,' Bridget continued, oblivious. 'But I realised that in a small community like this great value would have been placed on her fertility. Essentially, without being able to have children, she has fewer prospects.'

'Yeah. It's a crappy situation. You save her life on one hand but condemn her with the other. Sometimes you must feel like you can't win.'

Surprise flitted over her face.

'That's precisely how it feels. Every time. No matter how many times I see awful things happen to innocent people.'

'I'm not sure that feeling will ever go away, Birdie,' he said quietly.

'Neither am I,' she admitted. 'But, actually, I'm not too unhappy about that.'

'So tell me, Birdie,' he asked abruptly, 'what happened in your past to make you run away to help people in countries as far away from home as South Sudan, Nepal and Haiti?'

CHAPTER SEVEN

BRIDGET VALIANTLY TRIED to restart her heart, which appeared to have stopped beating. But it was impossible with what seemed like this spiked *thing* penetrating her chest.

The noise of the small party had faded fast into the night and all she could hear was a rushing in her ears. Then silence.

The worst thing about Hayden's question was that he'd asked it as though he actually cared. As if she really mattered to him, when they both knew that they'd agreed there was—and never would be—anything more between them.

'Who said I was running away from anything?' she choked out at last.

'I'm a commanding officer in the army,' he pointed out almost kindly. 'I've seen plenty of soldiers and civilians alike who have been running away from something. I can recognise the signs.'

'You're mistaken,' she said in a panicked voice.

'No.' His voice was so low that she had to strain to hear him. 'I am not.'

A charged energy arced between them and Bridget was forced to acknowledge that it was futile pretending to ignore it.

Worse, a part of her *wanted* to talk to him. She'd spent over a decade quashing her past and yet, with one seemingly solicitous question, she suddenly longed to tell him what he purported to want to know. As though sharing her story could somehow, finally, make it seem less defining.

But she couldn't speak.

The words simply weren't there and the silence lengthened between them. The seconds ticking slowly by.

'You can't run forever, Birdie,' he murmured at length, the compassion in his voice startling her. 'If you don't want to talk to me, at least find someone to talk to. There's no hiding place from who we are. At some point you're going to have to face whatever it is if you want peace. Trust me.'

'I don't have anything I need to face,' she managed. 'I have peace. Out here.'

'You have purpose out here,' corrected Hayden. 'That isn't the same thing.'

'So everyone is running from their past?'

'No.' He didn't rise to it. 'But *you* are.'

'You don't know as much as you think you do.' She bristled. But it didn't stop her from realising that there was truth in his words. And what did it say about him that he could read that truth in her, when no one else had ever done so in all these years?

'I know that you're a different person out here. Even if Mattie hadn't said so, and even if I hadn't heard all the things people had to say about you today, I would have known it from the way you became so animated any time you discussed your work when we were back home.'

He'd been talking about her to other people? All day? She wasn't ready to scrutinise what that meant right now—if it meant anything at all— but she could file it away for later. For when she wasn't feeling so shocked.

'That's just a passion for work. You're the same, by all accounts.'

'But you're a whole different person out here. Freer. Happier. Like you've undergone a complete metamorphosis.'

Freer.

Wasn't that the very word she'd used when she'd thought about it herself?

Her heart, which had started beating again at some point, was now pounding wildly in her chest. Clattering behind her ribs.

'I don't want to do this,' she muttered in a stricken voice. 'Not now.'

Though she noted that she didn't say *not ever.*

Hayden regarded her for a moment, and then he dipped his head simply.

'Then we won't.'

'We won't?' she echoed weakly.

It was that simple?

'We'll talk about what I'm going to be doing for the next few weeks around the clinic,' he continued smoothly. 'Work-related topics that won't make you feel uncomfortable.'

And what did it say that she wasn't sure she liked that superficiality either?

'You're going to be working around the clinic?' she managed. 'I thought your purpose out here was to survey the area around the vast training ground the military has been gifted? I understood that your *quid pro quo* was to put in some road and light aircraft infrastructure so that the region won't be so cut off and isolated when the rains come and the ground becomes a quagmire?'

'It is. But the mission has been extended to include some wat-san work.'

Water and sanitation?

'You mean like inspecting old boreholes that have stopped working around the region? Maybe stripping them down and rebuilding? Checking the generators?'

None of which would mean he was right on site, where she could round a corner and bump into him at any time.

'That…' He dipped his head in acknowledgement. 'But also we've been asked to construct some flood defences for the clinic. The idea is that we'll dig a series of drains around the old town to allow for expansion from the facility you have now into a main hospital once the buildings of the former town have been repaired. The drains will gravity-feed water into a four-or-five-metre-deep soakaway.'

'I see.' She tried to swallow past the lump in her throat.

Nerves.

She'd psychologically worked herself up to be within a few hundred metres of the army camp but knowing he could be working right outside the clinic felt like a whole different matter.

And wasn't that the problem?

She'd known from the start about Hayden the playboy. He'd even warned her himself. But still she'd let herself become too emotionally attached somewhere along the line—and she suspected she knew precisely where that *somewhere* had been.

Was she now supposed to walk around camp acting as though she knew him no better than anyone else? Bridget wasn't sure she could handle that.

'Where have you gone, Birdie?'

His voice snapped her back into the moment and her eyes flew to his.

'Sorry. Did you say something?'

If she didn't get a hold of herself then this was going to be the worst three-month medical mission of her entire career.

'I asked how your first few days have been?' he forced himself to ask casually. 'If it's different from other projects you've worked on?'

And he absolutely wasn't wondering whether she had been thinking of him as much as he'd been thinking of her, because that made no sense.

None at all.

He still didn't understand what it was about this particular woman that fascinated him so. He might have enjoyed flings from time to time but he'd never had, or wanted to have, a full-on relationship either.

Before now he hadn't even considered it.

So what made him want to get behind those defences of hers and understand what made Bridget Gardiner tick?

Wasn't he the one who talked about lines in the sand? About leaving their night of intimacy back in the UK, and focusing solely on a professional relationship out here? The way he wouldn't have had any trouble doing had it been any other woman. Then again, he probably wouldn't have given in to the temptation back home had she been any other woman.

And now wasn't he the one blurring those lines?

As if to prove his point, Bridget cleared her throat, clearly pulling herself together.

'Okay, well, the last week has been eventful. More frightening, draining, and sadder than I'd imagined it might be. Every other camp I've been to has had a small operating theatre and at least one surgeon, but this time we haven't had even that. I don't think I fully appreciated how many extra lives we could save with just one more tent and one more medical professional. And yet...'

'And yet...?' he prompted when she hesitated, keen to get them back to a more stable point, though he couldn't have said why it mattered to him so much.

Or perhaps he could have said so if only he'd cared to admit it.

'It always feels so satisfying when we manage to succeed. Even when we've had to endure losing three others, four, more, that one life we managed to save makes it all bearable.'

'I can understand that, Birdie.' He reached out to touch her cheek, but stopped himself. 'So, what are you all working on now?'

She narrowed her eyes at him.

'Why are you doing this?'

'Why am I showing an interest in your part of a joint charity-military project, do you mean?' He arched his eyebrows.

'Don't be facetious. You know what I meant.'

The worst thing was that he did know, and he wasn't at all sure what had got into him. He would never be so interested if it was anyone other than Bridget talking to him. But the fact remained he did truly want to hear about what she was doing, and how she was.

'I want to know how you are, Birdie. We might be drawing a distinction between our personal lives and our work lives, but that doesn't mean I can't ask about you. About how you are.'

'So you're saying you really want to hear about my day?' she repeated sceptically.

'I really do.'

And he didn't care what that said about how blurred his so-called lines were becoming.

'Okay,' she began slowly. 'So, the main problems we get out here are complications during birth, water-borne illnesses, and one of the biggest diseases we're dealing with here is *kala azar*. It isn't something you learn about back at home, but other people told me it was a major issue out here, so I researched a little. Still, I didn't realise quite how many of our patients would be affected.'

'I don't think I've ever heard of it,' he admitted. Although, having been on operations in so many different countries, he'd heard of many diseases, even if he didn't fully understand them.'

'No, it isn't something you really study back in

the UK.' Bridget exhaled, her passion and empathy twisting inside his chest. 'Another name for it is visceral leishmaniasis and, similar to malaria and mosquitos, kala azar is a parasitic disease spread by the bite of a sandfly.'

'That's concerning.' Hayden frowned, trying to concentrate on what she was saying, and ignoring the inexplicable urge to draw her into his arms. 'Sand flies are so tiny they can even get through the mesh on a standard mosquito net.'

'Exactly. And it develops slowly with initial symptoms being fever, swollen glands and an enlarged spleen, which basically lowers the healthy red blood cells, platelets and white blood cells in the bloodstream, leaving the victim prone to more infections, which, in a place like this, is like inviting any number of sick buddies to the party. TB, malaria, diphtheria, malnutrition, cholera, measles...the list goes on.'

'So I would guess that it's usually the complications of other illnesses that bring them to you, rather than the initial symptoms of kala...what did you call it?'

He might not know this particular disease, but he'd worked in enough areas to know the score. In places like this, hours' or even days' walk from medical help, from foreigners who the locals didn't necessarily yet trust, it was often too late by the time people sought help.

'Kala azar.' She tilted her head. 'And yes. The

later symptoms usually include anaemia, severe wasting and/or anything else I mentioned. Left untreated, most cases of kala azar prove fatal.'

Sadness burned in her eyes and he wondered how many cases she had seen already to look that way. And how old the sufferers had been.

Not for the first time, he was grateful for his job. He didn't envy Bridget—or his sister, Mattie, for that matter—the job of working with the sick and dying out here.

'But if they came to you earlier—' he tried to sound positive '—is the treatment straightforward?'

Bridget shook her head, her eyes slamming into his. As if they were doing more than simply discussing her medical cases. As if they were *connecting*.

'Actually, not really. The drugs are expensive to start with, but they need to be kept between two and eight degrees at all times, which is obviously a challenge out here.'

'Today was forty degrees in the shade,' he agreed.

'Right. And the treatment is usually anything from two weeks to over a month of intravenous or intramuscular injections on either a daily or once every two days basis. On top of all that, the drugs can have serious side effects.'

'It just gets better,' he commented dryly, as Bridget pulled a face.

'Doesn't it just. As if they don't have enough to deal with. And that's without the contraindications of different treatments the patient might need for the other diseases I mentioned. Or, if they're anaemic, the need for blood transfusion.'

For a moment they didn't speak, but it didn't feel awkward. It was an oddly comfortable, companionable silence as they pondered the situation, both acutely aware that they got to walk away in a few months. A luxury not afforded to the people forced to live in the region.

'Good evening, Bridget.' Bridget jumped at the sound of her project manager's voice. 'Major.'

'Hayden,' Hayden corrected with his trademark smile.

And good grief…was that Mandy actually giggling like a schoolgirl?

'Hayden.' She smiled broadly. 'Lovely name, my dear.'

Bridget blinked in shock. She knew Hayden was a charmer, but a bold, forbidding, often matronly woman like Mandy? From one single word?

'I'm not interrupting, am I?' Mandy looked from one to the other.

'Not at all,' they both said in unison. Which hardly made their case.

Mandy, known for missing very little, eyed them with mounting interest.

'Do you two already know each other?'

'I used to work with Mattie.' Bridget didn't know why she panicked to explain herself. 'That is, Major Mathilda Brigham, Hayd's sister...'

'We've been introduced before.' Hayden cut across her simply. Not unkindly.

She cast him a grateful glance.

'I see.' Mandy peered at them a little closer, and Bridget was sure she could see the wheels spinning in the older woman's head. 'Well, that make things easier in terms of working together.'

Bridget's heart kicked up at the idea, though she struggled to rein it back.

'I didn't think we *would* be working that closely,' she tried to say airily, though she wasn't entirely sure that she succeeded.

'It wasn't the original brief,' Mandy acknowledged. 'But Jukrem is such a new camp we didn't know what to expect in terms of footfall or types of cases. The longer we've been in the area, the better idea I think we're getting.'

'Did you have a particular project change in mind?' Hayden asked, getting straight to the heart of the issue.

By Mandy's expression, Bridget could tell the older woman liked his directness.

'Your right-hand man—Dean, is it?—was good enough to pass on the copies of the satellite images of the area that you guys brought out with you, as well as the geographical aerial surveys your team took today with their drones, looking for any riverbeds, wells or reservoirs. So thank you for that.'

'My pleasure.' Hayden smiled again, his charm not dipping for an instant, and even Bridget felt herself reacting. Again.

'I'm super-excited about the potential water sources, of course, and I know you've been tasked to focus on building infrastructure north of here up to the main camp of Rejupe, but I wondered if you were up for making a little detour?'

'How little is *little*, Mandy?' Hayden teased good-naturedly.

'Little...medium little.' She pulled a wry face.

He shot her a glance and she had the grace to look abashed. Bridget was shocked. She'd never seen Mandy look remotely accountable to anyone. But Hayden had managed it.

'So *medium big*, then?'

'Medium medium' was apparently as much as Mandy was prepared to admit. 'The thing is, those images also showed me that there appears to be a bit of a makeshift camp about half a day's drive south of here where the people have had no direct route to our medical centre during the rainy season because there's a wide riverbed between us.'

Hayden's brow knitted together. Not exactly a frown, but close enough.

'Forgive me if I'm wrong, but now the rainy

season is over and the river is already drying up, they'll be able to get to you soon enough.'

'Precisely,' Bridget cut in, unable to stop herself. 'The moment the river dries out completely and they can cross, they'll flock over in their droves, all at the same time. We'll be overloaded here in this tiny clinic. And we'll be at risk of any number of contagious diseases coming over as well.'

'Which you're here to treat anyway,' he countered. 'Or am I missing something?'

Bridget cast a quick glance at Mandy, who gave the tiniest inclination of her head, allowing Bridget to proceed.

'Yes, but what would be best is if we could get to them with a small outreach team before they come here. That would help us keep Jukrem and this other camp separate whilst we treat any different illness or strains of illness. It will reduce the pressure here. And because we've gone to them, we can step the consultations so not everyone is clamouring for our attention at the same time.'

'I was also thinking of sending a small distribution team, as well as a small medical team,' Mandy said earnestly. 'It might be a good opportunity to do it with the security of your team on the ground.'

But this time Bridget felt the older woman was addressing her more than Hayden. As though she thought that Bridget might have some kind of sway.

She tried not to feel flattered. But it wasn't working.

'We don't have a mandate to engage if there are any problems,' Hayden pointed out, but Bridget could tell he was open to suggestions.

He *wanted* to help them. She just had to give him a reason he could sell to his superiors.

'No, of course not. We realise that,' she hedged. 'I think Mandy's just hoping that the added bodies out there will be enough of a deterrent.'

'That's exactly what I'm thinking,' Mandy concurred brightly, but Bridget's eyes were on Hayd.

She watched him closely, knowing he was assessing the practicalities. She could see his side, but she could also see what Mandy was trying to say.

'The thing is,' she waded in again, 'there are a lot of refugees beginning to come into the area now that the rains have ended and the roads are starting to become usable again. Part of our role is to distribute non-food items, such as tents, blankets, cooking pans, even soap to them so that they can live.'

Mandy nodded—silent permission to continue. So Bridget did so.

'Obviously, at times like this, these are valuable items that can be stolen and sold on for a good price. So it's important that we only distribute them to the refugees who really need them and won't want to sell them on.'

'Which makes distribution a security risk,' Hayden concluded, catching on quickly, not that Bridget was surprised. 'Stealing, rioting, stampedes?'

'Right. We try to keep information scant so that our arrivals are a surprise and no organised groups have a chance to get there and pretend to be refugees. We take a few hundred kits each time. And we try to do it at night so that we can get to anyone who might have to leave early in the morning to walk a couple of hours to their jobs.'

'Then can I leave you to discuss it, and hammer out any details?' Mandy asked. 'Bridget here has worked on enough projects that I'm happy she has a good grasp of the situation. And clearly you two already know how to work together. I think appointing you as the liaison instead of Lisa is going to be the best choice on this occasion.'

And with that, the older woman moved away briskly. On to the next concern on her neverending list.

'I'm sorry.' Bridget pursed her lips as she watched Mandy leave. 'I didn't mean that to happen. I'll have a word with her later.'

'It's just a task, Birdie,' he answered casually.

'I thought you wanted us to keep some distance?'

'That doesn't mean we let it interfere with the job in hand,' he countered. 'Besides, I think we would work well together.'

'Do you?'

'Are you saying you don't think we would?'

Yes. No. Whatever. That was exactly what she was saying. Because it was now abundantly clear to Bridget that she, unlike Hayden, couldn't sleep with someone one week and then act normally around them the next.

Or maybe that was because it was *Hayden* she'd slept with. It wasn't as though she had anyone else to compare it to.

She felt trapped. As blocked in as this vast, landlocked country, and just as full of conflict.

'No,' she lied. 'Of course I'm not saying that.'

He grinned broadly and she knew that she'd just walked into that one.

The oddest thing was that she actually agreed with Hayden that they had the potential to be a good team. She happened to think so too. It was galling that the fact that he'd seen her naked and so…exposed had robbed her of the ability to act like she wanted to around him. Like the professional that she normally was.

Well, that stopped now.

'All right, let's discuss the feasibility. I think

an army presence will just give the illusion of additional security without you having to act on anything. And I know it would be a morale boost for the teams.'

'Teams?'

'A logistical team and a medical team,' she elaborated. 'I would be going on the distribution mission anyway as a medic, in case something were to go wrong and someone ended up getting hurt.'

Hayden frowned, something shifting in his gaze. If she hadn't known better, she might have thought he was actually concerned for her.

But that would be nonsense. Hayd was a self-confessed playboy who had slept with army officers who put themselves in danger on a regular basis. He wasn't going to around worrying about the her security just because…well, *because*. Bridget rushed on quickly.

'But also I've been told that, a few months back, Mandy had been talking about sending out a two- or three-man medical team in order to carry out a measles vaccination campaign if we were going to be out in those villages anyway.'

'Measles?'

'I know it's not a major problem back home, but out here it's second only to kala-azar in terms of serious paediatric illnesses,' she told him earnestly. 'It hits under-fives very hard, and unfortunately even with prompt diagnosis and our care, many, many of those children simply won't survive it.'

'And vaccinating them will prevent that?'

'It will give them a better chance than they would otherwise have,' Bridget confirmed. 'Certainly out here, where immune systems can be non-existent given the conditions. A mass measles vaccination campaign is something that I've done before elsewhere, but we didn't think we'd be able to here because of the security concerns.'

'Is that so?'

'Come on, Hayd.' The teasing tone was out before Bridget could stop herself. 'You know you want to help, deep down.'

She couldn't identify the look he shot her, but it made her stomach pull tight and heat pool between her legs.

'Okay.' He nodded. 'You've sold me. I'll put a dozen or so men together to accompany your teams. We'll put it to regiment as a support task as part of our mission to support the charity.'

'Thanks. I'll prepare the gear tomorrow. I'll drive the medical team in one of the charity's four-by-fours, and I'll get Christophe to drive the logistic team in the other. We can be ready to head out the day after.'

'Those timings work,' he concurred. 'But, Birdie, you'll need another driver. You'll be travelling with me.'

CHAPTER EIGHT

IT HAD BEEN a hectic night.

Bridget had been on call but hadn't slept well—if at all—and not just because of the conversation with Hayden. She'd lain on her bed, worrying, right up until a teenager had been brought in with a soaring fever. She'd had to strip him and administer a cold water sponge bath and paracetamol, before carrying out a malaria test.

She'd barely got back to her mosquito-net-protected bed, pretending that she wasn't still dwelling on the way Hayden had looked at her every now and then. When their conversation had flowed and he'd suddenly let his guard down.

And she'd schooled herself each time she'd risked imagining Hayden in his own hammock right then, in the army camp barely a couple of hundred metres away, on the other side of the wide but shallow dried-up riverbed.

Then the radio had crackled into life again. This time for another kid with fever but also convulsions. All tests led to cerebral malaria. Which meant stripping, cold baths, rectal paracetamol and plenty of fluids, along with an IV of diazepam.

The cases rolled in, one after another, and Bridget worked through each of them in turn. Methodically.

Oral rehydration and an overnight IV for one little boy, and skin-to-skin contact with the mother for an hour or so for another hypothermic little one. Then a snake bite, probably from about five days earlier, which meant it was probably a dry bite with no envenomation. Bridget assessed the site. There was no emergency but there was certainly a risk of infection, so she administered a tetanus booster and prescribed antibiotics.

But now they were in the army four-by-four as Hayden himself drove the two of them in the second vehicle.

'I didn't think you were allowed to drive yourself,' Bridget said as she slid into the passenger seat of the four-by-four, and Hayden swung into the driver's seat. 'I'm sure Mattie once told me that an officer had to have a driver.'

'Generally that's the case.' Hayden lifted his shoulders. 'Mainly because in the event of an RTA, an officer would have to go in front of a brigade commander if they were driving. Which isn't good for your career.'

'What if the RTA wasn't the officer's fault?'

'It doesn't matter,' he told her casually. 'If the

only contact you've had with a brigade commander is a disciplinary, even for something as unfair as an RTA that wasn't your fault, when it came to a promotion, that could be all it takes for them to pass you over in favour of the next guy on the list who has nothing going against him. Especially if you're talking promotion to Major or above.'

'So why would you take the risk of driving now?'

'We're in the middle of nowhere. There are no roads and few vehicles. An RTA is more than highly improbable. And, frankly, I'm damned good at what I do. If my brigade commander wants certain, specialist roles carried out, he comes and talks to me directly, he doesn't even bother with the charade of going through my commanding officer.'

'Modest,' she teased, unable to help herself.

'I've never pretended that was one of my traits.' He flashed his teeth in another of those wicked grins that melted her bones.

She struggled to hold herself together, searching blindly for a more neutral topic.

'Here's one thing I didn't fully understand,' she managed. 'The charity I work for has hundreds and hundreds of medical camps all over the world. How did the army come to be involved in this one?'

'It's a *quid pro quo*,' he answered. 'The government of this country gave the British, American and Canadian armies access to a one thousand square miles training ground on the basis that we help with infrastructure in the surrounding areas, after so many years of their civil war.'

'But how did that come to involve this charity?'

'You were already in the area, doing an incredible job with health, water, education. It made sense, rather than come in and do the same things that you guys do but not have the trust of the local people, to instead come in and support you guys, boosting your resources and manpower, enabling you to reach more people, faster.'

'Right,' she considered. 'And build roads.'

'And bridges. Yes. Like you said the other day, the rainy season has made everywhere impassable for so long that everyone has to move at the same time around here. People, cows, goats. Permanent roads will allow for freedom of movement throughout the year.'

'But that's going to take months and months, surely? Even years?'

'You appreciate that my guys can build a bridge in under ten minutes?' he asked, amused.

'Sorry? Ten minutes?' Bridget blinked at him, and suddenly all he wanted to do was stop the vehicle and pin her up against the beaten-up seats, tasting that luscious mouth of hers again.

'You mean…something like a little foot bridge?'

It took a herculean feat of self-restraint to keep his hands—and his body—to himself.

'No, I mean something like a man portable medium girder bridge that can span a nine-metre gap and support up to seven hundred and fifty tonnes.'

'Then with machines, surely? Tanks?'

'You're thinking of light armoured. No. I mean eight men.'

'And…you can set up one of those in under ten minutes?'

'We can when we're not under enemy fire. Takes a bit longer when my men also have to fire back.'

'Now you're being facetious.' She frowned.

How was that possible to make him want her more than ever?

'No, I'm just teasing.'

'Well, I hope you're enjoying yourself.'

'As it happens, I am,' he confessed with another grin. 'But wait until we get to our first river and you can see for yourself how we do it.'

'You're really serious, aren't you?'

'Like I said,' he told her breezily, 'this is something we have to do regularly, even in contact situations. If the rest of the army needs to move somewhere fast, we have to be able to make it happen.'

She pursed her lips, clearly tempted to agree. He could almost read the reservations as they paraded through her mind.

'Relax, Birdie. It will be fine.' He shrugged, ignoring all the alarm bells clanging in his head.

They'd been ringing ever since he'd heard himself tell her, the night of the welcome party, that she was going to be driving with him rather than in her own charity's vehicle.

Since when had he ever wanted to spend time with a woman so badly he was willing to bend the rules?

The answer—should he have admitted it rather than ducking the unspoken question entirely—was…*never*.

So much for concentrating on the incredible show being carried out less than twenty metres in front of her—so slick, so elegant, and so well rehearsed that it might as well have been a West End performance—all Bridget could think about was the fact that Hayden's leg was pressed sinfully close to hers.

She felt like a tangle of nerves and nothing else, leaving her jumpy and restless. Hayden, on the other hand, looked completely relaxed and at ease.

'So, right now the guys are putting together a

five-bay, medium girder bridge which can span a nine-metre distance, and once fully built, ramped and decked, can take up to one hundred and thirty tonnes if it's a wheeled vehicle, or if it's a tracked vehicle up to eighty-five tonnes.'

She tried not to consider the fact that the glorious early morning sun was painting the sky a stunning, cloudless blue whilst she was standing here with Hayden, leaning on the bonnet of his four-by-four, feeling utterly peaceful.

'Tracked vehicle?' It was a tousle to drag her mind back to the matter at hand. 'You mean… a tank?'

'Tanks, armoured personnel carriers, mobile platforms for high-velocity missiles.'

'You lost me after *tanks.*' She laughed weakly. 'But put it into context for me. What do tanks weigh?'

'On average? I'd say about seventy tonnes.'

'So you're telling me that those eight men out there can put a bridge in place in under ten minutes and it will get a tank across a nine-metre gap.'

'Steady on.' Hayden grinned, and her stomach flip-flopped all over again. 'They can put the bridge together in that time, but it takes a bit longer to push it out over a gap. Okay, so the initial part of the bridge you can see there is called the horseshoe, and the smaller part you can see at the front is called the nose. The pieces you can see each two-man team picking up right now weigh about two hundred kilos. But those beams over there—we call them bank seat beams—weigh around five hundred kilos each.'

'So that's why you guys suffer so many musculoskeletal injuries.' Bridget laughed, but it cracked at the end when her mind decided to suddenly conjure up an image of Hayden's body and the tiny scars she remembered seeing that night at his hotel.

The scars she'd touched, and kissed, and tasted.

'Yeah, they're quite heavy bits of kit.'

'Hmm?' Guilt lanced through her as her mind whirred. *Something about heavy bits of kit?* 'But your guys are making it look like a walk in the park.'

She shifted position, moving against Hayden. Everything sizzled through her. Working with Hayden was thrilling but simultaneously fraught.

Every time she thought she was succeeding in dampening the attraction between them, he said something, or did something, and it flared up again.

Exciting, yet wholly inappropriate.

'How do they actually get the bridge over the river?' she asked, valiantly working not to be distracted.

'They use the nose as a counterbalance and simply push it out.' He used his hands to try to demonstrate. 'Once it's fully across, they'll jack it down and begin decking it.'

'And you really built these bridges and used them whilst under fire?'

'Sure. But out here we can be quite casual. In theatres of war we'd be wearing body armour and all that kind of thing. It makes progress a whole lot harder out there.'

'So if you're here to build roads and bridges, why don't you simply leave the bridges you're building now in situ?'

'Honestly? Because we only have a few man-portable bridges here, so we need them with us. The idea is to put down more permanent bridges once we've finished assessing the area.'

'How will it get in?' she frowned. 'By road? Isn't that a bit of a catch-22 situation?'

'We'll probably have it parachuted in,' he said. 'With the country being land-locked it's going to be easier to fly over than to try to drive everything across potentially hostile terrain.'

'Oh, my word,' Bridget cried suddenly, jerking up to watch the men. For once her attention was where she wanted it. 'They're done.'

She didn't miss Hayden consulting his watch. Checking their time, making his mental notes, no doubt. Ever the OC. She smiled to herself.

'Will you have to collect that bridge again once we've crossed?'

'No, we'll be heading back so soon that we might as well leave it in place.' Then he grinned, pushing off the bonnet of the four-by-four and hoisting himself inside.

'Come on, Gardiner, let's go and save a few lives.'

They reached the camp in good time and in the end over six thousand families received plastic sheeting and blankets, food and a jerry can.

'Good morning's work,' Hayden commented, as they helped the logisticians pack up their now empty vehicles and begin the trip to Jukrem camp.

'Very good morning,' said Bridget happily.

Although she had been setting up her medical twelve-by-twelve over near the shade, and hadn't been needed for the distribution because of how smoothly everything had gone. And being away from Hayden had helped her to regroup.

'Now they've got something to protect them from the elements, to eat, and to collect clean water from the pumps already in the area, and from the new ones when you've drilled the new boreholes.'

'And you're good to go?'

'I just need to hang a flag.' She waved a well-worn but well-looked-after piece of cloth in one hand. 'And I'm waiting for an extra table that one the carpenters of the community is making for me.'

'Then you're doing the measles immunisations.'

'Yeah, but depending on take-up, my team is also hoping to screen for malnourished kids.'

'There's a test for that?' He looked surprised and she didn't blame him.

'More like a band for measuring mid-upper arm circumference.' She rolled her eyes. 'Not very high-tech, but it works. If the arm is in the green part of the band the kid is healthy—in the red and the kid urgently needs to be admitted to one of our hospitals. If it's in between they don't need urgent hospital care but they do need treatment.'

'And you're expecting red?'

'Actually, no. It's the end of the wet season so the cows and goats are healthy and producing plenty of milk at the moment, so the kids are usually well fed and fall into the green category. At least, that's what I'm hoping for because we're now heading into the leaner season. The next harvest isn't due for a few months so there's a bit of a hunger gap.'

'Right, well, you go and immunise or screen. I'm going to see if I can't find some liquid gold.' He tapped the survey map in front of him.

'Okay.' She laughed. Surprisingly happy. 'See you later.'

Like they were a couple. And the strangest thing about it was that Hayden didn't react to it at all. He merely shot her a smile and lifted his hand.

Her heart stuttered, though she told herself she didn't know why that would be.

'What is it?' he asked, as if reading her mind.

'Nothing,' she lied, her mind racing. 'Just, maybe, take some of the local builders with you and see if you can't teach them about gradients and gravity-fed soakaways.'

'Say again? I don't want to be patronising.'

'That isn't being patronising.' She frowned. 'It's acknowledging a reality. There are things they build or make out here that we wouldn't have a clue about, at least I wouldn't. Like baking their own bricks for construction, or the way they build those beautifully crafted *tukuls*. In the same way, whilst we understand water and gradients, it's currently new to them.'

'I see.' Hayden looked thoughtful but unconvinced.

With anyone else she might have left it there, not wanting to press her point. So what did it mean that she barely thought twice about explaining herself to this particular man?

'Listen, you and I might think putting a gradient on a pipe is intuitive, but it isn't, it's a learned technique and out here people haven't yet had a chance to learn it. They just think that because water flows, it won't matter in which direction, up or down. Our water, sanitation and hygiene expert has spent the last few days explaining the importance of putting a gradient on pipes or drainage channels but the simple truth is that she's a woman so they find it hard to believe her.'

'Will your WSH expert really want me taking over, then?' Hayden looked sceptical. 'Won't that just make it worse for her?'

Bridget offered a light shrug.

'Don't take over, then. Work with her instead. Whether we like it or not, it's just the way it is out here at the moment and we're here to help, not to judge or tell them they need to change. Change can happen in its own time—we can't force it.'

'I see.' Hayden looked thoughtful again. 'Okay, I might have a few experiments I can use to highlight the point. Leave it with me, I want to run it by your WSH expert first.'

It was all she could to stifle the broad smile that suddenly threatened to spill over her face. She really needed to stop reading so much into so little.

It was all she could do not to skip back to the medical tent. But as she stepped through the flap, expecting everything set up ready for the immunisations, she was confronted with a grim-faced colleague and a local woman at the end, blood all over the bed.

'What's going on?' Bridget hurried forward.

'Emergency.' Her colleague lifted her hands into the air. 'Her family brought her. We told them she couldn't come in here, but they carried her in anyway. She gave birth quite a few hours ago but the placenta still hasn't come out.'

'Okay.' Bridget nodded. 'She's going to need manual removal.'

It wasn't ideal as the place had been set up for measles vaccinations and there was no way they could use it now. But these women were well accustomed to giving birth at home, so if she'd come here then there had to be a real issue.

'Can you bring me long-sleeved gloves?' she asked, reaching into the boxes for a gown. 'Damn, no long gown.'

'No long-sleeved gloves either,' her colleague apologised, handing her a pair that covered hand and wrist only. 'These are all we have.'

Bridget fought to keep her expression neutral in front of the already worried family, but there was no denying it was an issue. She would need to insert her arm into the woman's uterus, sweeping the blade of her hand around the side in order to find the plane where the placenta met the uterine wall. Then try to manually work the two apart. But that meant inserting her arm right up to the elbow, and without latex gloves that was going to be a problem.

'What if we cut up several pairs of gloves and

kind of arrange them around my arm in overlapping rings?'

'We can try.' Her team looked dubious as one of them lowered her voice. 'Do you think I should get her family out? They're here to donate blood if it's needed to keep her alive, because if she dies, she would not only leave her beautiful newborn an orphan but also its four siblings. And the family, as much as they might care, simply wouldn't have the means to take on four young children.'

It was an added pressure, but one that was painfully familiar.

'We'll do our best.' Bridget nodded without looking up, her focus solely on cutting the fingers out of the gloves. 'But get the family outside and take their blood for cross-matching.'

A few minutes later the family was safely outside whilst Bridget slid her arm into the uterus and felt around for the placenta.

'I've got it,' she confirmed. 'It's free at the back but still attached anteriorly... Wait... There.'

Feeling it sheer off the uterine wall and fall, she slipped it out easily and the job was done.

It was going to be a successful mission. She could feel it.

CHAPTER NINE

HAYDEN COULD SLEEP on a clothesline. Over a decade and a half in the army had allowed him to perfect that technique. But tonight he couldn't even lie still. His thoughts were keeping his mind on a veritable assault course because he couldn't pretend he wasn't feeling this sleek, warm thing that moved around inside him every time he was with Bridget.

It was a madness, he knew that. Just as he knew he needed to put an end to it.

Yet he couldn't seem to be able to.

The rational part of his brain tried to pass it off as little more than a *sex* thing. The fact that no man had ever touched her the way that he had done, had even slid inside her, meant that she had given him the most precious gift indeed. It was only logical that it should have brought out a primal response in him.

But it was more than that—more than just the physical. It was as though she made his life better, brighter, more vibrant, even though he'd thought his life had been just fine as it was.

And that was part of the problem.

It was making it impossible for him to distance himself from her the way that he should, because really what could he offer her in return? A life like his mother had led whilst he lived his army life as his father had? Who would want that?

Yet if he tried to explain it to anyone, he wasn't sure they would have understood. How could they when his parents had appeared to have a happy marriage? And had loved each other?

Other people hadn't seen what he had. Those moments when he'd caught the utter loneliness in his mother's expression before she'd smoothed her face out and smiled at him with so much love that it had been blinding. He could still recall the first fifteen years of his life—Mattie was much younger, of course—when his family had moved once or twice a year, following his father up and down the country for each new posting and promotion.

He and his mother had felt as though their entire lives were a series of packing up, moving, unpacking, trying to make new friends, him trying to fit into a new school and his mother trying to find a new part-time job, finally settling in only to be told to pack up and move again.

But that was a road he didn't want to go down. Not now. So he found himself sitting by the fireside, chatting with the locals about nothing less beautiful than the carpet of stars that shone so brightly over their heads.

He'd learned how their names for the stars and the constellations differed so greatly from his own, and how their changing, flowing appearance throughout the year corresponded with the water missing from the sky during the rainy season, and the sky refilling during the dry season.

In turn, Hayden had answered their questions on why the moon was full some nights, yet not even there on others. And how the moon wasn't a great bowl that was lit up from the inside at night, as some of them had been taught to believe.

But now he sat, still and watchful, and finally alone, as the reason for his apparent insomnia crept silently out of her tent and came to join him by the fire.

'I heard you out here earlier, but I didn't dare come out whilst the elders were here.'

'Indeed,' he managed, unable to drag his gaze from her as she settled prettily beside him. 'Shouldn't you be getting sleep before your main vaccination day tomorrow?'

'Probably,' she agreed mildly. 'How did the drilling go today? Did I hear you were planning on building a high tank where the water could be chlorinated before collection?'

'I thought that if we could increase the chlorination we might be able to reduce the number and severity of Hep E outbreaks that seem to occur in this region. Then again, there was a study carried out a few years ago that considered the likelihood of recontamination by the water bottles used by individual households before they even got the water back home.'

'What were the results?'

'I don't know.' He grimaced. 'I couldn't find them published anywhere. But I could rerun the tests if I use turbidity meters, chemical analysers.'

'Is that in your brief?'

'No,' he confessed. 'But I considered recruiting and training some locals to help us collect data in the field.'

How odd that her approval should affect him as it did.

'That's a good idea, Hayd. The locals really appreciate being taught new skills that can benefit their community. It makes them feel far more valued that if they had to simply stand by and watch others—outsiders—doing it for them.'

'I figured as much.'

'Sorry.' She looked sheepish. 'I guess you already know that. You must have worked with communities before.'

'A few times.' He smiled. 'But don't worry about it.'

For a moment they fell silent, each of them

staring at the stars and losing themselves in their thoughts.

'Can I ask you a question?'

He didn't know why it made him tense, but he heard the forced note in his voice as he tried to tease her.

'Pretty sure you just did, Birdie.'

'Very funny,' she told him dryly, making him begin to ache.

As ever. As always.

'Fine, go ahead.'

'Why do you have such a reputation as a playboy?'

He paused, taken aback. Not that he was about to let that show.

'Do you really want me to demonstrate for you here? Now?' he teased. 'I'm more than offended you can't remember, of course.'

'My point is that I can't work out how you seem to have the time for all these women.'

'Why does it matter to you?'

'It doesn't,' she denied, unconvincingly. 'I was just curious.'

'Well, you know what curiosity did to the cat, don't you?'

'Then I've nothing to worry about, have I? Since, according to you, I'm the Bird.'

He didn't know why that should make him laugh, but it did. Hard, until he felt better than he'd felt in a while.

And closer to Bridget. Again.

He laughed for quite a while before an odd, sobering feeling began to creep up inside him.

'I don't know how my reputation came about, Birdie,' he managed softly, staring at the stars. Not addressing her directly. 'But I've always thought it was convenient for me. The perfect foil for the women who seem to think a single army officer must be on the lookout for a permanent companion.'

'But why?' she pressed. 'Whenever Mattie has talked about her childhood, it always sounded fine. Like your parents had a good marriage, and home life was great.'

And Hayden didn't know what it was, but something inside him...*shifted*.

'Mattie doesn't know what she's talking about sometimes,' he exhaled softly.

'She said they were happily married for twenty years before your mother passed away unexpectedly. She has always wanted to emulate your parents' marriage.'

'Well, she shouldn't. My sister isn't in possession of all the salient details.'

'Such as what?'

Hayden slid his gaze to her, this woman he didn't need to see in the darkness to be able to picture every line and angle of her lovely face, this woman who had slid under his skin when he hadn't been looking. And he heard himself begin to speak.

'My parents' marriage wasn't quite so perfect in the beginning, but Mattie's too young to remember, and I've never discussed it with her.'

He stopped, wondering why Bridget, of all people, should be the first person he had ever talked to about this. Giving her the chance to speak. But she didn't, she just sat watching him steadily and there was something encouraging about that.

'You know my father was a soldier? Yes, well, we got posted to different places a lot. Every nine months or so we'd move house, up and down the country, but because my father was away on exercises, it was my mother—and later me, too—who would have to pack everything up, clean the old home before the army would come and inspect the house and march us out, and then get to the new house and unpack everything.'

'That must have been difficult.'

'New home, new school, trying to make friends, every nine months.' He gave a ghost of a smile. 'Yeah, it was tough. But it was harder on Mum. Mattie was just a baby, and because we were always moving—not even always to where my father was, if he was on exercise—she didn't have a support network of friends and family. She couldn't have a career, although I think she would have liked one, she just had to find a part-time role to fit in around Mattie and I. And all the responsibility for family was on her.'

'I can't imagine,' Bridget said quietly. Sincerely. And he loved how she could convey such empathy without sounding either patronising, or gushing.

'She became depressed. Nothing suicidal, but meandering through mild to moderate depression, then back to being okay. Sometimes the house would be a tip. All the time. She could barely get herself moving. And other times she was so on top of it all that not a single thing would be out of place, and I'd almost be afraid to touch anything.'

'You're right, this isn't what Mattie has ever known.' Bridget shook her head gently.

'Like I said, she was a baby. By the time she started to get to the point where maybe she might have started to remember, my father got a promotion, and a more permanent posting in HQ. He was home a lot more. As in, every night. Everything changed.'

'She wasn't raising a family alone.'

'Right. She had support, and Mattie was older, so she actually went out and got herself her first job as a receptionist at a dental practice. It seemed to give her freedom and a new release. And that's the family life that Mattie remembers.'

'But it isn't the one you remember most?'

'No, it is.' He shifted in position, looking for the right words. 'I remember that, and I look back on it with affection. And although, looking back on it, Mum was clearly depressed, she kept herself together for the sake of Mattie and me. Home life was never miserable, and she was a good mum. A great mum.'

'But...?'

'But I remember how difficult it was for her because of my father's army career, and I think that any woman who wanted to be with me would have to put up with the same kind of stuff. I'm a soldier, it's who I am. I get moved around a lot, and I'm always away on exercises, or training, or operations. It's a great life for a single person. But my personal opinion is that it isn't conducive to good relationships. Or happy marriages.'

'I don't know,' she said thoughtfully, after a moment. 'I think it's different, Hayd. Or it *can* be different. You don't have a family, and not every woman is like your mum. What if you chose a woman who was also in the army, and career-minded like you?'

Or a medical charity worker, posted abroad for months.

The thought hung there in the air, and Hayden was sure Mattie could read it as well as he could. But he didn't say it.

'Then we'd never see each other.'

'That isn't true. And, even if it was, in time

you would get promotions, and be offered more roles that gave you a more permanent situation, instead of postings here, there and everywhere.'

It was astounding how much he wanted that to be true. And how much he wanted it to be true with Bridget.

'It isn't just that, though,' he made himself continue. 'It's also the nature of what I do. You see my unit building roads, drilling boreholes, digging drainage channels. But that isn't all we do. We also deal with mine warfare, explosive demolitions, anything. How is it fair to settle with one person knowing that in the next operation you go on, you might never make it back?'

'It's admirable that you consider others,' she told him quietly, firmly. 'But that's not a choice you should be making on their behalf. That's a choice each individual should be able to make for themselves.'

'I disagree. There's often a romantic notion attached to what we do, and that notion is often a far cry from the reality. I *know* the reality, I've lived it. I've stood next to a best friend one moment, only for them to step on a land mine and be gone—literally vaporised from existence—a second later as we turn away from each other.'

And if he'd expected his resolute, focussed Bridget to drop her eyes from his even as she dropped the topic, he should have known she was stronger than that.

'Maybe you should try trusting people a little more,' she told him evenly. 'You might be surprised at what they've experienced themselves. And just how much they understand. Often more than you might think.'

How he stilled himself in that moment Hayden would never know. Every nerve ending in his body was on fire just keeping himself from crossing that invisible divide between them and hauling her to him.

He'd kept telling her there was a line between personal and professional, and that what had happened between them back in the UK could be kept separate from what happened between them out here.

But he suspected—more than suspected—that it was himself who he kept trying to remind. *He* was the one who, after years of being happily single and never wanting more, couldn't keep his mind from wandering back into territory it shouldn't be in.

Imagining Bridget. Like he had no control at all where she was concerned—she dominated his every waking moment. And, if he was honest, she haunted his sleep, too.

He told himself that it was just temptation. Purely a physical attraction. Undeniable chemistry. But whatever term he tried to use, the fact was that it was still here, hovering like a ghost in the periphery of his mind.

No matter where he was or what task he was on, a part of him was always aware of where she was and what she was doing. He could never shake this *longing* to go to her and talk to her. Touch her. Take her.

As if she could make him forget everything he'd ever thought was important in his life if he only gave her the chance. The thought was more frightening than he could have imagined.

And something else besides that he didn't care to examine in that moment.

Suddenly he didn't want to talk any more. He just wanted to act. Reaching out, he slid his hand behind her head and pulled her easily to him, his lips brushing over hers for a fraction of a second before he tilted his head and claimed her mouth with his.

Hayden was kissing her. *Again.* And it was even better than all the memories she'd been replaying in her head these last couple of weeks.

He was unrushed. Unhurried. Tasting her and sampling her, as if he'd never done so before. They said you could never experience a second first kiss, and yet this felt crazily close.

It was like he was pouring more into that kiss than she'd known before. More of *himself.* Telling her things with every scrape of his tongue, every slick move of his lips. Hot and demanding.

Only she was afraid to believe them, in case she was reading too much into the unspoken words.

So, instead, she just gave herself up to the kiss. Submitting to the sensation of his calloused thumb pad against her cheek and indulging in the magic as if it was a spell from which she never wanted to be released.

She had no idea when she moved, or even that she had, only that suddenly she found herself against him, wrapped in his arms with his chest hard against hers. He kissed her over and over, his hands cupping her jaw, his fingertips gliding softly down her neck, as if he couldn't get enough of her.

As if she was the most precious, beautiful thing he'd ever held. And then he kissed her some more, licking his way over her lips and kissing a path down the line of her neck. Heat bloomed right through Bridget, as her skin seemed to grow taut over her body in some kind of visceral response. Like her insides were liquefying and he was turning her core molten. She was sure that if he hadn't been holding her so tightly, she would have fallen in a puddle, right there on the hard ground.

As it was, she was helpless to control the greedy little sounds that kept escaping from her. She couldn't stop her mind from spinning in some dizzying, glorious, calamitous waltz that could only end with her either soaring to vertiginous heights or crashing agonisingly on the ground.

He moved his hand lower, his palm raking over her tee, making her skin prickle with the need to feel his touch. Lower still, until suddenly he was covering her breast with his palm, his thumb grazing over the tight bud. All she could do was arch into it as a kind of jagged wildness ripped through her, leaving her wanting more. *So much more.*

Vaguely she heard the alarm bell in her head, warning her that if she didn't stop now she wasn't going to be able to and for a split second she froze.

Hayden pulled back instantly.

'Hayd...' she whispered, the loss of contact leaving her feeling bereft.

'No.' His voice was ragged, like glass. 'You were right to stop. That should never have happened.'

'Not here anyway,' she managed weakly.

'Not anywhere,' he corrected, and she hated the grimness in his tone.

Hated that he regretted the kiss they'd shared. Because as much as she knew they couldn't have continued, she couldn't quite bring herself to wish it hadn't happened.

She wanted to tell him that, but the moment was gone. Lost forever. And as he stood up, hauling her to her feet beside him and settling her before taking a clear step away, she knew that there was no trying to reclaim it.

Her heart was beating hard and fast in her chest. The simple truth was that Hayden had convinced himself a long time ago that he didn't want a woman in his life, and if he was ever going to change his mind then he needed to come to it in his own time.

On the other hand—she vacillated as she so often did when it came to this man—it was worth remembering that just because he'd confided in her about his childhood, it didn't necessarily follow that *she* was the woman he would ultimately want.

If anything, it was possibly somewhat arrogant of her to believe that she held an allure for him that no other woman who had gone before her had held. And yet…the flame of hope flickered in her chest.

'I should go back to my hut,' she murmured eventually, trying to eradicate the shake from her tone.

Pretending that it wasn't a fight to keep her distance from him.

'You should.' His voice was clipped, and still she didn't think she was imagining that undercurrent.

'I'll see you in the morning,' she added softly.

He dipped his head once in silent affirmation, but she knew instinctively that he wouldn't be in camp when she woke. Maybe he would drive to the site of another potential borehole, or perhaps he would head off to conduct more ground surveys of the area. Either way, he would be putting a bit of distance between the two of them.

And as much as Bridget told herself that was a good move—a wise decision, given that that ever-shifting line in the sand—she couldn't help feeling that Hayden was fighting her for all the wrong reasons.

That maybe he was trying a bit too hard to tell her that she didn't mean anything to him.

CHAPTER TEN

'WILL SOMEONE CALL the doctor again, and tell him this is an emergency?'

Hearing Lisa's frazzled voice from outside the emergency *tukul*, Bridget hurried over. It had been a frantic few days since she'd returned to Jukrem camp, her measles vaccination programme a success. And in some respects Bridget had been grateful for the bustle to distract her.

She'd suspected that she wouldn't see Hayden after that kiss they'd shared a few nights ago, and she hadn't been wrong. But now, far from lamenting it, Bridget felt it had been just what she'd needed. She'd still been shaking over the sheer intensity of it up until yesterday. Seeing him could only have made things a hundred times more intense.

'Can I help?' Bridget asked, pushing open the plastic screen that served as a door. 'I can…'

'Stop.' Hewa, a local nurse trained by the charity, hurried to the door to block Bridget's way, but Bridget's attention was already dropping.

Down to the floor and the blood-soaked earth. Then the blood-covered shoes of the nurse.

'Retained placenta,' Lisa told her grimly. 'Baby is okay, she's over there. But the placenta didn't come away even though I tried the usual procedures. And then she started haemorrhaging.'

Carefully sidestepping the blood, Bridget made her way to the bed where a young woman, lay, the life literally draining out of her.

She couldn't focus on that, though. She could only focus on Lisa.

'Did you run a manual removal?'

'I tried,' confirmed Lisa. 'I ran the usual procedure of sliding my hand in to run the blade of my hand around the uterus... I did it to the letter, Bridget. But it's stuck fast, she's still haemorrhaging and there's nothing I can do.'

'Is the placenta abnormally deeply embedded?' Bridget asked.

'Abnormally,' Lisa echoed with a nod. 'Yes.'

'Okay, so we can't risk anything more, she's going to need surgery. Hewa, can you get this girl's relatives together to see if they can donate blood? Lisa, de-glove and clean up. Then maybe see if you can get a bucket to try to catch some of this blood before it hits the ground. No point having us slipping and sliding as we try to treat the poor woman.'

Usually a birth was a glorious event. But

not right now. Not when the beautiful, healthy baby the midwives had just delivered was lying, swaddled but untouched, his mother only metres away, unconscious, and at any moment could need to be resuscitated.

As soon as she could, she would look to get something to clean up the blood that was already all over the delivery room floor. It wasn't going to help anyone to see it, let alone anything else.

Janet appeared just as Bridget was passing the door. The doctor was sweating in the forty-degree heat and looking like she hadn't been to bed for days. Bridget knew exactly how she felt.

Being here was utterly demanding, but it was also fulfilling.

'You radioed me?'

'Patient with retained placenta. It's abnormally deeply attached, and our patient began haemorrhaging.'

As Janet entered the delivery room to see her patient, Lisa began to run through her actions to correctly detach the placenta.

'Okay, so it's embedded in there,' Janet confirmed at length. 'Let's give her fluids and something to get her blood pressure up before she crashes.'

'Right,' Bridget concurred, all too aware that the blood pressure medication was potent.

They were going to have to count the drops to infer infusion rate as it was going to need very careful titration. The sooner she could get donated blood from any suitable relatives, the sooner they could start to reduce this incredibly powerful blood pressure medication. But the fact remained: the placenta was embedded and they didn't have the means in this camp to get it out.

'Surgical solution,' Bridget muttered. 'Meaning transfer to the main camp at Rejupe?'

'Only choice,' concurred Janet. 'But I'm afraid I heard the heli was on a run elsewhere. And there's no other way.'

'What if she could be driven?'

'The ground is still too unpredictable. Not all the riverbeds are traversable.'

'And if the army did their bridge-building stuff…? I saw them when we went to the outreach camp. They're fast and direct. It's probably this girl's only chance.'

For a long moment Janet considered it. Her mind working on one problem whilst her hands worked on another. The biggest concern was that their patient was going to start bleeding into her uterus.

'Go,' she urged Bridget abruptly. 'Speak to the OC. If he agrees, we'll leave straight away.'

Stepping outside, it took a mercifully short time for her to locate Hayden, engaged in discussion with one of his men, a set of plans in front of them.

Hayden was poring over a map when Bridget called his name.

It was probably a good job, as his mind was so active that he couldn't have seen a single contour line or feature if it had leapt up and engaged him in a fist fight.

He made himself turn slowly, willing the few days away to have dulled his irrational reactions to her. But when he saw the expression on her face, everything else dissipated.

'What's wrong?' he demanded. 'What do you need?'

'We've an emergency,' she told him without preamble. 'A young mother we have to get to the main hospital in Rejupe for immediate surgery. We've requested a transfer, but the helicopter is already on site elsewhere.'

'So you need us to head out along the route and lay any bridges or sections to ensure you get a smooth run?' he surmised.

'It would save us hours and ensure our safety.'

'And the patient?'

She looked him straight in the eye, causing that habitual flare of electricity.

He stamped it out.

'We can carry her in the back of a one of our four-by-fours, but we're going to have to carry mobile monitoring equipment, rig up some kind of pole for the IV, and ensure she has a medical escort with her as well as a driver. That means needing room and, more importantly, tying up two of our staff.'

'I'll give you a couple of drivers and a four-tonner,' he said without preamble.

'Thank you.'

He glanced quickly at his watch 'When do you want to go?'

'As soon as possible. The longer we wait, the more chance she will bleed out into her uterus. We just need to get a medication pack for transport and make any last-minute infusion changes.'

'Who is the medical escort? A local nurse?'

He didn't know why he asked. It wasn't as though it made any difference.

'I don't know,' she replied, but there was the faintest hint of a blush under her tanned cheeks. Not that he knew what that meant. 'Probably a local, yes. Though it should be someone who can handle a critical care situation like this, and who will know how to deal with any possible complication that may arise *en route*. But we can't spare any of the doctors. They're all needed here.'

'Sort your medication pack, I'll jury rig a pole for your IV line to the canopy of the four-tonner. When you're ready to bring your patient out, my guys will come and carry your stretcher.'

'Understood,' she confirmed. 'Thanks.'

And then she was gone, and he was striding to the mess tent to find his second-in-command, to hand over command. Logically, he didn't need to go. But a trip to Rejupe camp would be a good opportunity to get the lie of the land, especially as it was a main site.

And that was the only reason, he told himself obstinately.

'Hey, Dean, just need to brief you,' he stated, walking into the ops post.

'What's up?' Dean asked, looking up and seeing he was alone.

'The charity has just asked us to assist with a cas-evac to Rejupe. I'm going to need a four-tonner and driver for the patient and medical escort, along with their mobile monitoring equipment. Also, an MGB on a DROPS, with an eight-man team.'

The DROPS would be the perfect vehicle to carry the Medium Girder Bridge.

'What's the lead time?' Dean asked, already going through his task sheets.

'They're ready to transfer the patient, timings are on us, of the essence. Send a runner to use the charity's radio and find out what billets will be available at Rejupe, so let's go for an O group in fifteen minutes to let the guys know what gear they need to bring.'

'Understood. I'll also let Lieutenant Johns know that he's going to be your second-in-command while I'm gone. It'll be good practice for him.'

'Better let him know he'll be *your* second-in-command.' Hayden deliberately held his tone neutral. 'You'll take command here while I head to Rejupe. With it being the main hospital and camp, I might as well do the recce we were planning to do there next month anyway.'

'Makes sense,' Dean agreed, taking it at face value.

'Great, right, I'll go and grab my kit and be back for the O group.'

He heard Dean answering over his shoulder, but Hayden was already heading out of the ops tent, telling himself that it was business. The mission.

Nothing more.

'How's the baby doing?'

'Hungry,' Hayden growled, ignoring the amusement in Bridget's eyes as she watched him trying to cuddle the newborn.

She'd basically shoved it…him…into his arms as soon as her patient's stretcher had been carefully manoeuvred onto the vehicle amongst the equipment, ignoring his objections. Not that he'd many the moment she'd told him that the baby's mother was all the kid had, his soldier father having been killed by a rebel group a few months earlier.

It was a point that had served to remind Hayden how the country's civil war had raged for so long that even now the peace they had was painfully fragile.

'I'm really not sure that I'm the best person to look after him.'

'You're fine,' she'd answered in a tone that had invited no argument. 'I need to have my hands free for the mother in case anything goes wrong. And babies around here don't get put down, they're held all the time, even if it's in one of those intricately woven newborn baskets the women carry on their heads.'

'I'm not carrying him in a basket on my head,' he'd said with a grimace.

Not that Bridget had seemed to care.

So now he was stuck holding a baby—literally—whilst watching her deal with any problems with her patient, as their vehicle made careful progress along what didn't even pass for roads around this place. And he found himself drawn in by the way Bridget kept talking softly to the unconscious mother in what seemed to be quite a decent grasp of the young woman's language.

Caring.

Then the baby began to grouse again, causing him to have to start the jiggling and soothing of his own all over again.

'Sing him a song,' Bridget suggested.

'Say again?'

'Babies love songs, right?'

'How the hell should I know?' he demanded, but it lacked any real heat. 'And I don't sing.'

'Well, you'd better start now.' She chuckled as the baby had made its objections even clearer. 'Either that, or show him the birds outside by the river, or the purple lily beds, or the sorghum in the fields.'

'Egrets.'

'Sorry?' She frowned at him.

'The *birds* you mentioned are egrets. Yellow-billed egrets, to be more precise. They nest in the trees along the riverbank at night.'

'I didn't know that.' She rocked back on her heels, surprised. 'Although I *do* know that the river in this area offers good fishing opportunities, especially at this part of the season, right when the locals are caught between the rainy season and the next harvest.'

'So I understood.' He laughed, loving the tiny glower it earned him.

How was it that he'd come to relish those moments more than anything else? Because those were the times when she struck him as being the most *herself.*

'We're not far out now.' She peered around the back of the vehicle and out at the landscape, which was, to be fair, rather boringly flat.

As everywhere was in these parts.

'About an hour by my calculations.' He checked his watch.

Again she poked her head out the back and peered around.

'I'd say a little longer. There's something of a deceptive dip in the terrain around here. Takes you by surprise if you're not careful.'

Yes, he knew all about things around these parts taking him by surprise. He was staring right at one of them. Two, if he counted the precious being currently nestled in his arms, so tiny that it was almost fragile.

Almost.

He'd been around them long enough to hear that cry and know that these babies were a lot more robust than they seemed.

'Are you really hating this?' she asked suddenly, taking a break for a moment from checking her patient.

'Hating what? Doing a recce in the middle of our training ground that I was going to be doing anyway?'

'You know what I mean.' She dropped her voice until, even in the back of a four-tonner, it felt almost...*intimate.* 'Being in the back of this lorry, holding a baby.'

He pondered her question for a moment, almost tempted to lie, before wondering why he needed to.

'Let's just say that I'm disliking it a lot less than I thought I would,' he answered honestly, and then, as if to prove the point, he found himself peering down at the baby to check he was all right, before snuggling him tighter.

As if he was somehow protecting this tiny, fragile bundle from the potential of becoming an orphan in the next few hours.

'Quite a compliment,' she told him, and he couldn't tell if she was serious or not.

'Maybe our patient here will call her baby *Hayden*.'

For a moment she looked bleak, and he didn't need to be a doctor to know that the chances of the mother surviving were low as it was, and getting lower with every moment. Not that his drivers could go any faster with the sick patient on board.

Then Bridget gathered herself together and made herself answer. And he liked it that she kept her voice upbeat and her words positive, even though they were both fairly sure that the mother was too far out of it to hear. And that, even if she could, she wouldn't be able to understand.

'Maybe.' She forced a smile.

And she didn't contradict him.

For a long, long while they continued in silence.

'You'll like Rejupe,' she told him at last. 'My team acclimatised here for a couple of days before we headed out to Jukrem. Unlike back there, where we have hole-in-the-ground latrines, the guys here all have individual bathrooms, plus they live in purpose-built accommodation blocks. It isn't five-star but it's plush compared to where we are.'

Not that she would be anywhere but Jukrem.

'Quite a luxury.' He matched her grin with one of his own and something delicious shivered through her. She tried to ignore it. 'So, what's the plan when we arrive?'

Bridget shrugged her shoulder but kept her voice deliberately even.

'Hopefully we'll get to the camp in good time, the surgeon comes out to assess, and they take her straight into surgery.'

'And then for us?'

She knew he didn't mean anything by the word *us*, but it rippled through her all the same. As if there was a possibility of that word meaning something more.

No, it probably wasn't what he'd meant at all.

She shook her head imperceptibly and tried to concentrate on the question he had more likely been asking.

'It will depend on how the surgery goes. If it's successful, Mandy suggested returning with our patient on the supply plane since it's scheduled to fly into Jukrem in a couple of days.'

'And if the surgery isn't successful?' he prompted gently when she stopped.

Her throat felt suddenly tight. She couldn't explain what it was about this patient or her baby that had got to her as it had. She saw plenty of sorrow and death in this job, and it was never easy to accept, but one grew accustomed to it.

What other choice was there?

'If it isn't…' she gritted her teeth '…then I guess I'll be returning with your team at first light tomorrow.'

'Understood.'

She nodded, forcing herself to remain upbeat for the sake of the mother and baby if nothing else. They might not be able to hear or understand her, but either way she wanted to keep the atmosphere around them a positive one. It mattered to her.

'So, at Rejupe we'll get to sleep in decent beds for a night or two, enjoy hot showers and eat food that doesn't come from a can. Maybe we'll even have the opportunity to go into the local town and buy some gifts for back home.'

For a moment he just watched her, making her feel as though her body was turning inside out. And still the word reverberated around her head. *Us.* Hayden and herself. Was it possible? Did she even want it to be?

'Sounds good.' He spoke at last. 'I want to speak with the project coordinator here anyway to get the lie of the land, so to speak, and then I think I like the idea of a hot shower. But maybe after that you can show me around this market of yours.'

Surely her body shouldn't so instantly thrill to the notion? As though a part of her was hoping for…what? A repeat of that kiss? Or more, such as a repeat of their night together?

And why not? a voice whispered in her head.

No matter how much she tried to avoid him—admittedly, she hadn't tried that hard at times—it was as though *fate* kept throwing them together, telling her to be bolder and have some fun. Again.

But then what? Where would it go from there?

Relationships out in places like this, in NGO camps in the middle of nowhere, weren't exactly encouraged. Back at training they were frowned upon, usually because any tension between the couple inevitably fed through to the rest of the team.

Then again, she'd known plenty of couples to hook up on missions and if both parties were discreet, putting their roles first and not allowing their relationship to make anyone else feel awkward, it went largely ignored.

It was just that she'd personally never had a hook-up. She'd never wanted to. Never even been tempted. Until now.

Until *Hayd.*

The devil on one shoulder was whispering that this was a second chance to break out of her usual shell. To pursue something with Hayden, safe in the knowledge that it couldn't last past the three months' time limit imposed on them by the date when he and his unit were due to return home.

She couldn't get hurt if she put a definitive end date on it. *Right?*

But the good girl on her other shoulder was reminding her that getting together with a colleague was a potential distraction. That she had a job to do, and that didn't include acting like some kind of lovelorn teenager around the brother of the woman who was—for all intents and purposes—the closest thing she'd ever had to a best friend.

The issue was that she didn't seem to be able to control herself where Hayd was concerned. That gave her two options. She could either roll with it and indulge in the attraction for the first time in…well, *ever.* Or she could consider removing herself from temptation altogether and ask the project coordinator for a transfer away from Jukrem—and Hayd—altogether.

Bridget knew what the logical solution was. So what did it say that it was definitely *not* the choice she wanted to be making?

CHAPTER ELEVEN

SEVERAL HOURS LATER Bridget was standing under the shower and simply revelling in the glory of the hot water rolling over her.

The handover had gone as well as she could have hoped, with her accompanying the mother as she'd been whisked into surgery, whilst Hayden—still carrying the baby—had been led to the neonatal ward.

The surgery had been promising and the team had done everything they could. Now it was just a matter of waiting. And hoping. And that meant enjoying the shower, which was nothing like the power showers of back home but certainly better than the solar showers she'd been having in Jukrem.

And pretending that she didn't feel wrecked by Hayden.

Why was it so impossible to shake the man from her head?

Refusing to give in to any more distractions of the six-foot-three variety, Bridget soaped up quickly, rinsed, and shut off the precious water supply. A bit of revelling was one thing, but even though the infrastructure here at the main town of Rejupe was better than at the mobile camps at Jukrem, she was still sensitive to the resources.

As she changed into a fresh set of clothes, Bridget raised her hand to the door of her temporary two-metre-by-three-metre room and promised herself a quick check on her patient's surgery, a bite to eat, and the first full night's sleep she'd have had in a couple of weeks.

So why was her heart hammering at the idea that she was about to embark on the closest thing to a *date* with Hayden, taking him into Rejupe town to sample the gastronomic offerings of the market, as she'd promised?

For a moment she debated feigning exhaustion and crying off. But then, suddenly, there he was, standing in the middle of the square in the charity's compound, waiting for her. His long, muscular legs stretched out in front of him, apparently oblivious to the two women crossing the area behind him, their eyes riveted.

'Ready?' he asked, taking a step towards her.

Her chest constricted. So tightly she could actually feel her breath squeeze out. All she could do was smile and nod, trying to keep steady as he fell into step beside her and they headed out of the gates together.

'I heard the mother's surgery went well,' he said after a moment.

'It did,' she managed, forcing herself to say more. 'We're waiting to see how she goes overnight.'

'Right.' He nodded, falling silent again and leaving Bridget to mentally kick herself for sounding so strained.

But she didn't need to worry, he spoke again after a few moments, sounding as relaxed and unconcerned as ever.

'Do you have anywhere particular in mind for eating?'

'Quite a few,' she answered gratefully. 'I'm trying to think of the best one. There are marketplaces in the main town and even pizza restaurants and a bar where the staff—foreign and locals alike—go to decompress.'

'Sounds great. I'll follow your lead.'

'Okay.' She grinned, and there was something about the way he wasn't trying to take control that made her relax that little bit more.

For a while they wandered around, soaking it all up, and Bridget found herself recounting some of the stories from when her group had last been here earlier in the month.

'What about eating here?' She stopped at last by some tables near a street stall she remembered, which showcased some of the tastiest local cuisine. 'There should soon be some entertainment in that open area opposite.'

'Here it is,' he agreed, looking around for a moment. 'Any recommendations?'

'Lots.' She laughed, the delicious cooking smells making her stomach rumble loudly. 'As you can hear. And it's kind of like tapas, so we can try plenty.'

'I definitely like the sound of that.'

So, a few minutes later, they sat at the table with a selection of little pots in front of them from which they both tried green beans flash fried with onions and garlic, dough balls with a variety of dips, and bowls of chicken with different sauces.

'This is a little better than the Friday night offering we have at Jukrem.' She laughed, popping the last mouthful of local cake, complete with a creamy frosting, into her mouth.

'Isn't it.' Hayden grinned. 'It seems like they have a whole host of stuff on offer on a Friday night. When I was in the neonatal ward I heard that tonight is movie night for them.'

She grinned, easily able to imagine that one of the single girls had invited him to join her there. But instead of accepting, he was here. With her. It made her feel...*special.*

'Yeah, they had that when I was here. No worries for them about conserving power and electricity shutting off from midnight onwards, like we have to back in Jukrem.'

'Evidently.'

'The guys here don't know what roughing it is. Did you know they even have their own cook?' She paused and cocked her head to one side. 'Wait, you guys have your own chef out in your army camp, don't you?'

'What can I say? The army knows how to live.' She loved the way he laughed.

'I thought I saw you with some local builders the other day, trying your hand at *tukul* maintenance?'

She tried not to flush as she thought of quite how she and, if she was being honest, a couple of the other nurses had taken the long route between the outpatient building and the wards a few too many times that day whilst Hayden and his men had been working.

'Maybe you can repair some of the huts back at Jukrem? Though probably not the large one, which was once the kitchens area, I believe.'

'No, that hut is definitely too far gone,' Hayden agreed. 'You're better off staying in the temporary kitchens in the twelve-by-twelve for now.'

'And the open stone barbecue, that's a decent cooking set-up.'

His eyes held hers over the table, making her heart pound for no reason other than it reminded her it was just the two of them.

'I'm not saying my guys will rebuild the entire *tukul* village, but I did think we might have a go at mud hut repairs before we go. Maybe get the army to fund us enough to employ some of the local builders, once we get back to camp, to teach everyone.'

'That isn't a bad idea,' Bridget mused. 'As long as you pick a new gang at the start of each week, you won't fall foul of the local labour laws.'

His gaze turned more serious.

'Good to know. I think the more we try to integrate and use locals, even in the construction of the roads, the better we're going to integrate into the area, especially when we've got full brigades here for training. Before we left Jukrem I discovered a couple of very traditional builders who still know how to build the ancient way, and *tukul* construction is quite similar to traditional Celtic roundhouse builders.'

'Isn't it like a woven stick—walls packed with mud?'

'It is, but they have a particular way to do it that ensures structural integrity. Enough to support the long conical poles that reach up to that crown in the centre. And the most intricate part is the stunning, handmade, local rope that binds it all together.'

'Did you learn to thatch it too?' she asked, Hayden's enthusiasm beginning to infiltrate.

'Not from the locals, although I have tried thatching before, back in the UK.'

'I tried that once back home, too. Maybe one day we could learn together,' she began, and then stopped.

What was she doing? It had been a throw-away comment that had made it sound like she was making plans for the future. Hayden must be cringing. They might have started to talk a little more, or it felt as though they had anyway—certainly recently—and things might seem good between them right at this moment, but that didn't mean she wanted to go ruining it by sounding as though she was pressing him for more than they'd already agreed. Or by getting too personal.

Hadn't he already told her that he didn't envisage seeing her again once they'd left this country? He had never suggested that getting involved in a relationship had ever been part of his plans.

But was tonight a tiny hint that he just might be changing his mind? No, she was probably only fooling herself, if she believed that.

'I meant the charity and the army could learn together,' she clarified awkwardly. 'Not just *you* and *I*.'

'I understand that,' he replied smoothly, much to her relief. 'The point is, I figured that rather than trying to repair that kitchen *tukul*, which, as you said, is a bit far gone, I might just rebuild it altogether.'

'Wow, that would be great.' She blinked, trying to clear her head. That unwelcome awkwardness from her blunder still lingering in her mind. 'Somewhere us charity workers can maybe eat together?'

'A bit more of a social space,' he agreed. 'And if that project goes well I was considering contacting HQ whilst you guys contact your team back home to see if we can't get the go-ahead to construct a small village in Jukrem. Once we've got in a few more fresh water stations, we'll know how the dwellings could be arranged for the best.'

'I think that's a great idea.' It was amazing how quickly he could make her start to feel at ease again. 'Jukrem is growing a lot faster than we'd imagined. It was only meant to be temporary, a bit more than a mobile medical camp, but certainly not the main medical hub that it seems to be turning into.'

He nodded as she warmed to her topic.

'But that's hardly surprising with its proximity to that refugee camp. And with more and more people flooding in every day, it really is a good outreach site. Now it needs to be more.'

'I agree.' Hayd dipped his head gravely. 'Now the rainy season is over, more displaced persons and refugees are going to start arriving *en masse*, by road and by river. If Mandy is on board as the charity's project coordinator, she is best situated to contact your charity's HQ.'

'Yeah, she is.' Happiness spread through Bridget and she couldn't pretend it was just at the thought of Hayd's team helping the charity. 'And she'll be delighted. So, these *tukuls* of yours, will they come complete with the wildlife?'

'Say again?'

'Well, mine came with a hedgehog, Lisa's has a mouse, and Janet's has a couple of lizards.'

'Hedgehogs, lizards, and mice...' He pretended to jot it down. 'But no spiders or cockroaches, I'm guessing? I'll see what I can do.'

It was nice, Bridget thought as they headed back to the compound an hour or so later, the way they could banter and take time together. They'd spotted some of the other staff in the town, along with a group of Hayden's men, all enjoying the unexpected downtime, with Hayden lamenting the fact that he was now going to have to ensure he sent all his men for a couple of days' R&R to Rejupe in the interests of fairness.

And then, all too quickly, they were back at the compound, walking through the gates together, and she had to tell herself that she was only imagining the fact that they'd both slowed down, as if trying to prolong the night that little bit longer.

She really needed to get a grip on herself.

Since when had she been the kind of person to read non-existent things into situations? Biting the inside of her cheek, Bridget made herself stay quiet as he walked her to her room.

'Well, this is me, then,' she managed, as she stood with her fingers on the handle, unable to make herself actually push it open.

'Yes.'

She wanted him to say something, *do* something, and yet at the same time she didn't. It was painfully confusing.

'I'll see you in the morning,' she managed stiffly, flinching with embarrassment.

He didn't answer straight away, and she didn't blame him. Who knew she had a long-hidden skill of turning a perfectly innocent moment into something insanely uncomfortable?

With a great effort she pushed the handle down and began to open her door.

'We could check out the film?' Hayd suggested brusquely, halting her.

It was incredible how badly she wanted, at that instant, to pull the door closed and go with him.

Go anywhere with him.

Bridget would never know how she managed to hold her nerve. How she managed to push that door wider. How she managed to make her legs work long enough to carry her those couple of steps inside.

'Thanks, but I think I'll get to bed. It's been a

long, long day and I haven't had a good night's sleep in a decent bed in what feels like forever.'

And she shut out the fact that every fibre of her being was screaming at her not to be such an idiot.

One more night, it cried. *One more night with Hayd before he goes back to Jukrem in the morning.*

'If you're sure,' he replied, his voice altogether too husky.

Too tempting.

His head was dipping towards her. Barely a fraction but enough to convince her that this time she wasn't imagining anything.

And, Lord, how she wanted to say yes *to whatever it was he might be offering.*

'I'm sure,' she rasped instead.

'Birdie…'

'Don't.' She shut him down before she could think. 'It would be a mistake.'

And then she slammed the door and pressed her back against it before she could do something stupid, like grabbing him by those all-too-solid shoulders and dragging him into her tiny room.

It took her a minute or so to catch her breath before she could push herself off the door again. Another minute to walk across the room to her bed, pull the covers back and then stand there, staring blankly at the sheets.

She wanted him. Incredibly, he wanted her

too. Just like he'd wanted her that night at the club. And the night they'd shared after that. And maybe that didn't mean they had a future together, but who said they had to have one?

Who said she couldn't enjoy just one more night with him? Because she *wanted* to spend another night with him. She wasn't sure she'd ever wanted anything quite so much in all her life.

Abruptly, her body working overtime before her brain could process what she was doing, Bridget found herself snatching her door open again and striding back into the corridor.

Striding back down the hallway and to his room, even though she had no idea if that was where Hayd had even gone. And then striding into his room before any could see her, having barely waited for his answer after she'd offered the tersest of knocks.

'Birdie?' Half a question, half a growl, his voice rumbled through her. 'I thought you said it would be a mistake.'

'The second one we'll have made in less than a month,' she pointed out shakily. 'But we still have next month to work together. And the month after that.'

'Do you have a point, Birdie?' he rasped. 'Or are you just pointing out my failings? Failings I never had, I should point out, before you came along.'

It was the most backhanded compliment she'd

ever heard, although she was sure he hadn't intended it as a compliment at all.

'I was thinking that I could ask to transfer.'

For a long moment he merely stared at her. His blue gaze darkened by the moment as he pinned her to the spot.

'Say that again?'

She ran her tongue over her suddenly parched lips and wished he didn't follow the movement so intently. It made her want things she knew she couldn't have.

'I could swap job roles.'

Bridget had absolutely no way to read what that almost infinitesimal shift in facial expression meant, she just knew it had happened. In the silence she heard herself adding more.

'If it would make things easier.'

And still Hayden didn't reply.

'It's just that, when I left our patient heading into surgery earlier tonight, one of the project coordinators was telling me that a new role had opened up in a different camp and she wondered if Mandy might want to send anyone from Jukrem to fill the gap.'

'And you volunteered?'

'No, I just…said I'd ask Mandy once we return. But now…well… I just thought that if I left Jukrem it might make things easier.'

'Do you want to leave Jukrem?' he asked simply, breaking the silence at last.

Everything tilted inside her.

'No,' she admitted.

She just hoped he didn't ask why, because she wasn't as ashamed as she should probably be to admit that that he factored into that choice more than he had any right to.

'I don't want you to leave, either,' he ground out instead, taking her by surprise.

Then, before she could answer, he strode across the room, cupped her face and lowered his mouth to hers.

CHAPTER TWELVE

AS EVERYTHING EXPLODED around her, all Bridget could do was cling to him. A thousand tiny detonations burst out of her like her own body wasn't enough to contain them.

His tongue invaded her mouth, scraping against her own, and she welcomed it. When he angled his head to deepen the kiss, she rejoiced in it. It was like her entire being was singing an aria that it only knew when Hayden was there to conduct.

But it wasn't enough, she wanted to be closer. Sliding her hands from his shoulders, she let her palms graze their way down over his rock-hard abdomen, tugging gently to pull them out.

Abruptly, Hayden wrenched himself away, leaving her feeling bereft and confused. But then he headed for the door, spinning a chair around and lifting it up in one hand as he went. Jamming it under the doorhandle and testing the improvised lock with impressive dexterity.

They weren't likely to get interrupted, but Bridget was grateful for his additional care.

And then he was back with her, his mouth fusing once more with hers and hands releasing her hair from its confines and tangling his fingers into it as he let it tumble around her shoulders. As if he couldn't get enough of her.

It was an intoxicating experience.

At some point, without her even realising it, his hands moved from her hair and over her body, like he was trying to learn its contours. The slope of her shoulders, the indentation of her waist, the dip in the hollow of her back. And then they were moving over her chest, testing the shape of her breasts through the thin tee, grazing her hard nipples with the pads of his thumbs and making them both groan a little in appreciation.

But as much as she arched her back, pressing herself into his palms in a silent plea, he seemed intent on torturing her. The sweetest torment she had ever known but a torment all the same, when all she really wanted was to feel his bare skin on hers, his hot, wet mouth closing over her aching nipple.

Again and again he teased her until she thought she would go out of her mind. Then, when she thought she couldn't take any more, he hauled the tee over her head, undoing and removing her bra in one slick movement. And then his mouth was closing over her, and Bridget thought she could burst with pleasure.

Need punched through her, hollowing right into her core. She slipped her hand into his hair, cupping the back of his head, her body arched into him. *This* was what she'd been missing. *This.* Right now. Wild sensations, and primitive.

And she wanted more.

Reaching for his clothing, the buttons, the zips, Bridget fumbled a little in her haste, and the curve of his mouth against her sensitive skin practically seared through her.

'We have time, Birdie,' he muttered, though she didn't answer.

She couldn't.

All the same, he let her push the jacket off his shoulders and then tug his T-shirt over his head until they were finally, gloriously, skin to skin. The hard planes of his chest feeling all the more muscular under the softness of her breasts, abrading her nipples and making her almost mad with desire.

All this time she'd been telling herself she'd built up that night with Hayden to be more than it had been. Now it was clear to her that she'd been downplaying it in her mind. So this time— on the basis that this was all there could ever really be between them—she was determined to preserve every perfect moment of it in her memory forever.

She dipped her head forward to kiss his chest. To taste him. To smell him. Sandalwood and musk, and something that was all Hayden. She moved slowly, thoroughly, determined not to miss a single inch of bare, solid, chest as she blazed a trail over him. His low murmurs of approval spurred her on. Making her drop to her knees in front of him as her chest tightened in anticipation, her breath coming in short starts just as his was. Particularly when she reached for his trousers and unbuttoned them.

'Bridget...'

It was a caution, but she didn't want to hear it. She couldn't quite understand what it was inside her that *wanted*, so badly, to do this. But it drove her on, making her curl her hand around him and draw him out.

'Shh...' she managed, her voice thick with expectancy as she felt a deep shudder course through his body.

And it was strange, wasn't it, the unexpected sense of power that instilled in her. How, even though she might be the one on her knees in front of him, she felt as though she held him in the palm of her hand. And not just literally. She smiled to herself, her lips curving along his hot, velvety length.

Then, lifting her eyes to his to make contact and hold it, she ran her tongue all around him and took him deep into her mouth.

* * *

Hayden had no idea how he managed to stay standing upright. He'd been pleasured before by women far more practised than his former virgin Birdie, yet never before had he experienced such a primal reaction as he did at that moment. His legs actually shook as though they might give out underneath him at any moment.

Her mouth was hot and perfect around him, but it was the shots of pure lust that jolted through him that pulled at him the most. Threatening to unravel him in an embarrassingly short time.

Desire and something far, far more dangerous coursed through his veins. And he couldn't bring himself to care. He couldn't bring himself to do anything but focus on her. *Birdie*. She was making him feel hotter, and greedier, than he'd ever felt in his life.

It was like he'd tied himself up in an inaccessible parcel all these years, but she was freeing him with every sweep of her tongue and each graze of his teeth. Teasing him one moment and worshipping him the next. Driving him closer and closer to the edge…until he feared he was going to topple off.

Hayden would never know how he managed to rein himself in, pulling himself out of her willing mouth and catching her off guard. Even when she rocked back on her heels, her wide eyes staring up at his in surprise, he feared he would still fall.

Before she could speak he was lifting her up, shucking off the rest of their clothing and carrying her to the single cot bed that surely couldn't take their combined weight. It didn't even look as though it could take a man of half of his stature.

But he couldn't let that stop him. *Them.*

Hayden had no idea what it was about Bridget that made it impossible for him to control himself when he was around her. But, then, he wasn't sure he even cared, just as long as he could taste her plump lips. Hold that incredible body against his. And slide inside her like he had over and over that night in the hotel.

Wordlessly, he pulled the mattress onto the floor and laid her down, almost reverently, on the clean white sheet he'd only put on it moments before she'd walked in and he'd proceeded to lose himself in every perfect inch of her.

Propping himself on one arm, he cradled her cheek with the other hand.

'That wasn't…good?' She blushed prettily.

'That was perfect,' he growled. 'But if I hadn't stopped you when I did, I don't know that I'd have been able to any later.'

'I didn't want you to stop me.' She glowered at him from under those long, thick lashes of hers. 'I didn't want to talk about it. I just wanted to…*do.*'

Insanely adorable, but he wasn't about to apologise.

'If you don't want to talk, Birdie,' he managed wryly, 'perhaps you'd consider stopping.'

And then, before she could object any more, he set about reacquainting himself with each long line of her and every delicious curve. Relearning her, as though it had been a lifetime since she'd last been in his bed. In many ways, it felt as though it *had* been.

He dropped his mouth, intent on kissing every inch of her satiny skin, all the while knowing that he couldn't get enough of her. He kissed, he licked, he grazed, revelling as she arched into him, seeking more. Demanding more. She began to move her hands over him on an exploration of their own. She let them glide up his arms and to his shoulders, before slipping down his back, using the leverage to arch up into him let her hard nipples rake over his chest and set him alight all over again.

And then she slid her hands lower, cupping his backside, and she opened her legs to him until he was nudging against her wet heat before he could stop himself. The heat outside was making the room that much hotter, and it was that much easier to slide against each other.

He heard a moan and wasn't sure if it had come from him or her. Possibly both. A dark, urgent need moved within him. A madness that he didn't think could ever be controlled.

'Please, Hayd,' she whispered. 'Now…'

And he was lost.

He'd told her that she'd come here to run away from something. But it had never occurred to him that he'd done the same with the army. Maybe he hadn't wanted to see it, or maybe it had taken these events to bring him to it, but the simple truth was that he'd been lost, and he'd only realised it when Bridget had found him.

Holding himself above her, Hayden slid inside her. Only a little way at first, then out. Then repeating it again. Slowly. Lazily. As if it wasn't killing him to do so.

'Deeper,' she gasped on a ragged breath, tearing down the last vestiges of his self-control.

This time, when he tried to slide into her slowly, Bridget gripped his backside and lifted her hips.

He drove home with a groan and all his ease and skill disappeared in an instant and the rhythm became harder and faster. He ran one hand up her silken thigh as she wrapped it around his back, letting his head drop until his mouth was pressed in the flawless valley between her breasts. And still the rhythm didn't let up.

The entirety of his long length was buried so deep inside her that neither of them knew where one of the ended and the other began.

As though it was *meant* to be that way.
Always.

When he felt her shift around him, he reached down between them and found the centre of her need, his fingers playing with her until she was gasping with every stroke. She clenched around him, arching right up off the bed and muffling her voice against his shoulder as she cried out his name, shaking deliciously around him.

And Hayden finally let himself go. Throwing them both into the fire and taking him higher than he'd ever been before. Higher, he feared, than he ever would again.

Bridget had no idea how long it took to come back to herself. She only knew that when she did, her body was still pressed up against Hayden's. Fitting to him as though they'd been hand-crafted to go together—as ridiculous as she knew that notion was.

A thousand questions hovered on her lips at that moment, but she didn't dare utter a single one of them lest it break whatever spell had wound its way around the tiny room.

She suspected that she wasn't alone because Hayden didn't speak either, he just held her close as if he never wanted to let her go.

Or perhaps she was just being fanciful. Perhaps that was why the confession slipped out of her.

'You were right when you told me that I used this place to run away. I didn't want to acknowledge it before, I don't think I was ready to do so, but now it seems far clearer.'

His pulled her closer, his hand drawing circles on her skin. Encouraging her to keep talking in her own time.

'I had a relatively privileged childhood. A nice house, a good school, lots of money, and we moved in quite elite social circles. Then, when I thirteen, my father was arrested for fraud. Every single thing we had was off the backs of other people, some of whom were meant to have been our friends.'

She loved that low rumble of objection from him, making her feel as though, had he been able to, he would have protected her. It helped her to continue.

'Overnight our whole lives were torn apart. Mine and Mum's. We were thrown out of our home, understandably, and all our assets were frozen. We had only the couple of bags we'd been allowed to pack, under the watchful eye of the police, of course, but nowhere to go. No one wanted to help us, or even be associated with us, since the media couldn't accept that my mother hadn't known about it.'

'Had she?' he asked gently, his arms still around her making her feel safe. Secure.

'No.' Bridget shook her head. 'I really don't

believe she ever did. My mother was very beautiful but not very worldly. At all. I truly believe she was foolish enough to fall for all the lies my father fed her, but the media didn't believe that. Or else they didn't want to. It was a national scandal.'

'I think I can believe it.' Hayden paused, and she tensed. 'Did your father take his own life before his trial?'

Nausea rolled through her, but Bridget fought against it. *She* was the one who had brought up this subject, she wasn't going to let it beat her or make her cower the way it had for the past thirteen years.

'Yep.' She tried to sound flippant. 'Mum and I were devastated. For all that he'd done, I was only thirteen and he'd been the father that I'd idolised my entire life. But Mum fell apart. My dad had been her whole life. She'd lived vicariously through his successes—although, of course, they were never successes at all—but she'd thrown all the parties, all the PR events, all the social functions for him. It was the only thing she knew how to do. He'd brought in the money—she'd never earned a penny in her life.

'And, worse, with Dad gone the media had no one else to blame. We were hounded. For years we couldn't go anywhere or do anything without someone recognising us. Mum became depressed, spiralling into one addiction after another. Losing herself in anything that could make her forget, for a day or a night. And I became her carer.'

'You don't have to talk about this if it's too difficult for you,' Hayden said tenderly 'But I'm here for you, as long as you need.'

Bridget nodded. It was tempting to stop, but she wasn't even sure that she could put the lid back on the proverbial box. She'd opened it up and memories and emotions she'd thought long buried had spilled out all over the place.

And somehow it felt good to be able to start to talk through it.

'I'd dreamed of becoming a doctor for as long as I could remember. I'd always been good at school but finding myself without friends had just given me more time to throw myself into my studies. At least schoolwork was always there for me and didn't care what my father had done. So I had the grades to go to university and study medicine, but I didn't have the money to support myself. Besides, I soon realised that I couldn't leave Mum.'

'Is that why you became a nurse?'

'I suppose. It brought in money to keep a roof over our heads, and it kept me in medicine one way, but it meant I didn't have to go away for my studies. When she died five years ago, that was when I became a volunteer.'

'You reinvented yourself,' he acknowledged.

'I can see why that would have been far easier to do if you were thousands of miles away from everything you'd ever known.'

'Crazy, isn't it?' she commented wryly. 'But I don't want to run away any more. Besides, ever since I met you, I don't think I've been running *from*. I think I've been running *to*.'

'I was wrong, Bridget Gardiner.' His voice slid over her like the honey that families here poured over their wounds. 'I don't think you run anywhere. I haven't thought that for some time. You stride with confidence, and you inspire wherever you go.'

'Even with you?' she asked, only half teasing.

'Especially with me,' he growled, making it sound altogether too much like an unspoken promise.

Before she could second-guess herself, she found herself pulling out of his arms to straddle him.

An echo of their first time together.

'Show me,' she whispered, spreading her palms over his chest and moving her hips over him, revelling in the way his body had pulled hard and tight in an instant.

For her.

'Your wish is my command,' Hayden growled, his hands moving to her hips to lift her up as though she weighed nothing and then settle her back where he wanted her.

Heat bloomed in an instant. And Bridget let her head fall back and be guided wherever he wanted them to go.

CHAPTER THIRTEEN

'WHAT'S GOING ON?'

The sun was just peeking over the horizon the next morning as Hayd's men lined up their vehicles at the compound gates and Bridget threw her grab bag inside one, trying not to glance at Hayden himself for fear that ridiculous emotions would be written all over her face.

Her body still ached lusciously from their night together. In truth, they'd barely been able to keep their hands off each other long enough for her to sneak out before anyone caught her, less than a few hours before.

Now they were due to head back to Jukrem, after deciding with the doctors at Rejupe that although both mother and baby were doing remarkably well, they would stay for a few more days to recover, before being brought back on the supply plane in the middle of the following week.

But whilst the Rejupe volunteers had been relaxed and calm an hour ago, there was suddenly a bit more of a flurry than usual, and before she could ask anyone what was going on, she saw one of the Hayden's men rushing over to speak to him.

'Sit-rep, please,' he ordered.

'Sir, there's been some kind of an attack at a camp called... Luerina.' The man checked his notes. 'No reports of casualties.'

Wordlessly, Hayden waved her over and she hurried around the vehicle.

'Do you know anything about the camp at Luerina?'

'Luerina is about two days' journey north of here,' Bridget replied. 'It's a small outreach camp like our own. If you think about a clock face, with Rejupe here at the centre and Jukrem in the seven o'clock position, Luerina is at about the one o'clock position.'

'Right.'

'You're sure there were no casualties?' She turned to the young man.

She knew volunteers who had gone to Luerina. People who weren't just colleagues but friends.

'None that we know of, ma'am, but our intel is sketchy. We've never had any communications in the area so the reports coming through now are through the charity. You'll probably know it from your team before we get the report.'

'Thanks,' Bridget acknowledged as she turned back to the door and jogged out over the courtyard towards the hospital cluster. The charity had their own communications facility, and the project managers here would surely have more information.

Her head was so full that she wasn't expecting it when Hayden fell into step beside her. But she wasn't surprised either.

'Slow down.' He placed his hand gently on her arm. 'It won't help anyone if you end up with a broken ankle.'

Reluctantly, Bridget slowed.

'Do you know the team?'

She bit her lip. It had to mean something that he could he read her so easily. Didn't it? A sob bubbled inside her, and she fought to choke it back.

'I know, I know,' he said softly. 'You're all out here for the same reason, working for the charity. I get it, it's like a brotherhood. Or sisterhood, if you prefer.'

Despite everything, she managed a wry smile.

'I understood what you meant.'

Reaching the hospital, she headed for the radio building where plenty of others were milling around, the volume louder than usual.

'What's going on?' Bridget asked one of the nurses whose face she recognised from the previous day, even if she didn't know her name.

Hayden had already slipped across the room, no doubt going to see if his men could lend support.

'Apparently Luerina got hit a few days ago. A couple of pick-up trucks of rebels. They got medical supplies, food and a charity vehicle, but fortunately no one got hurt.'

In the grand scheme of things that was, at least, some good news.

'And the guys who were working there?'

'They're all on their way here,' the nurse answered. 'The charity called them back straight away, until local police can apprehend the rebels. They still had another vehicle, so they were okay. We understand they're less than an hour out.'

Relief coursed through her.

'Thank goodness for that.'

'You're heading back to Jukrem with the army unit?'

'I'm heading back with part of the unit. Hayd...that is, the major in command, is taking a group of his men out on a recce into the area around Luerina.'

'That's good.' The nurse nodded. 'We could do with someone seeing what's going on out there. How many rebels there are and what they're after. The reports coming in are conflicting and no one is quite sure what the situation is.'

And Hayden was the perfect guy to do that. So why did her chest ache so badly? As if a part of her wished he didn't have to go?

'Anyway,' the nurse continued, oblivious to Bridget's unease, 'if you can wait just for an hour or so, I think the project coordinators are working out a group to send out with you.'

'A group of medical volunteers?' Her attention switched immediately back to the nurse. 'To Jukrem?'

'I think they decided that a bunch of extra medics at Rejupe wasn't the best use of resources. If we have that kind of skill on hand, and we aren't safe in the Luerina area at the moment, we might as well send a mobile vaccination team out towards Jukrem, maybe help alleviate some of the sudden influx you guys have been getting by intercepting those refugees closer to the border. Especially the mothers and babies.'

It was a great idea, and one that offered Bridget the perfect lifeline. The ideal distraction from worrying about Hayden going to follow up a group of rebels.

Being part of that mobile medical team would certainly help to refocus her on the job she'd always loved—being a nurse in places like this. And she had no doubt that once she spoke to Mandy back at Jukrem, the woman would be only too happy to send her with the team. Not least because it might help to take the pressure off them in camp.

'Sounds good. Think they'll need an extra pair of hands?'

'They usually do.' The nurse laughed. 'I should have been that quick off the mark.'

'Well, maybe I'll see you there.'

Jogging over to the comms unit to see if she could contact Jukrem and confirm her plan with Mandy, Bridget felt a little happier with herself.

Hayd would have a plan. She knew him well enough to know that. But now she had a plan, too. One that didn't involve sitting around and worrying about him.

She only hoped it would work as well in practice as it did in theory.

'This is Waeya. She's three years old,' the triage nurse told Bridget as she stepped around the makeshift bay in the mobile clinic her new team had set up near the refugee camp just over half a day's drive from Jukrem.

The plan had been a sound one. As anticipated, the increase in new refugees coming over the border had meant a significant uptake in the number of visitors to Jukrem camp itself, and Mandy had jumped at the idea of a vaccination team being able to get to hundreds of them sooner. Another week, she'd told Bridget, and Jukrem simply wouldn't be able to get through the backlog.

Even now, both Rejupe and Jukrem were recruiting and training both local nurses and healthcare providers in their scores.

In many ways, it was a compliment. Testament to how well their charity had integrated into the area and become a trusted source for the local people. All the teams in the region deserved to be proud of themselves. Bridget knew that she was.

And she wasn't remotely thinking about Hayden, and whether he'd been safe out there. Days away from camp. Days away from *her*. Or the fact that he'd apparently arrived back at the army camp near Jukrem the day before, in time for a parachute drop that night. She wondered if he'd even been across to the charity's camp, only to find out that she wasn't there.

Then she hated herself for even thinking about it. For even caring.

Because Hayden wouldn't care. It had been a one-off, that night. Logic told her that it didn't mean anything more than that.

As soon as that call had come in, he'd forgotten all about her, focusing on his job instead. *Exactly* the way that he was supposed to do. Just as she was.

And still something ate away inside her. The fear that she couldn't pigeonhole her emotions the way that he could. The fact that a part of her was ignoring every warning she was trying to heed, and instead it wanted more.

And Hayden had made it abundantly clear that he didn't have *more* of himself to give.

'Waeya's mother brought her in whilst you were away,' the nurse prompted, and Bridget snapped her head round instantly. 'She has coughing, chest pain, and is severely emaciated. She weighs about ten pounds. We've diagnosed TB and begun treating with first line oral antibiotics and second line injections.'

'*Male*, Waeya,' Bridget whispered to the oblivious little girl on the makeshift floor cot, the huge mosquito net pinned all around her. 'Mum's being screened now, is she?'

'She's right next door,' Lisa confirmed. 'Come on, I'll show you our last, new patient.'

'Here?' Bridget turned expectantly.

'Next door.' Shaking her head, Lisa led her out and across to another tent with a couple of white mosquito net domes inside, where a pulse oximeter was emitting an unwelcome beep, warning of a low oxygen level as it tried to help those infected little wet lungs.

'Hamar is eighteen months old. He missed his measles vaccination when his family fled their village after an attack. I don't know how many weeks or months it took them to make their way here, or when Hamar contracted measles.'

'You've treated him with oxygen to help his lungs and antibiotics for secondary infections?'

'Yes, but he continued to deteriorate so we tried a course of steroids and have finally seen an improvement. Right now, we need to ensure plenty of fluids and good nutrition, and salbutamol to ensure the lungs are open. But it looks as though we may have turned a corner with him, so right now we're holding onto that.'

For the next six hours Bridget talked the older nurse through their patients, concentrating on the information that was never at the briefings but which made such an impact on the ground. By the time she emerged, stepping into the wall of heat and shielding her eyes from the sun, Bridget wasn't expecting the large crowd jostling excitedly in the market area. Instinctively, she headed over. And stopped in her tracks.

Whatever she'd expected, it hadn't been to see Hayden crouched down, sifting through muddy, dirty water.

What was he even doing out here?

Emotions charged through her and she found herself heading over, a thousand questions dancing on her tongue. But when she spoke, even she didn't recognise the light, teasing tone in her voice. So completely at odds with all the turmoil coursing through her at that instant.

'Having fun?'

Hayden twisted his head to eye her critically.

'Bad day at the office,' he answered simply.

As though he hadn't been away. As though nothing portentous had happened at all. And maybe, for him, it hadn't. Bridget swallowed hard and fought to keep her tone airy.

'Is that so?'

He stood up, glaring balefully at a dodgy-looking generator hooked up to an even more unreliable-looking control panel, before turning to face her. And then, suddenly, he lifted up one arm and brushed a stray hair from her face with the back of his hand.

Like flipping a switch to let light suddenly flood the dark, needling void in her chest. Making her feel almost...*joyous.*

'Some group got hold of this old jenny, but it keeps pumping out mud and gunk along with the water, and the panel keeps giving people electric shocks. I figured I'd take a look.'

'Nice.' She grinned.

'Hardly.' He wiped his hands on the army-green rag from his pocket.

'Aren't you supposed to have men for that, *Major*?' she teased. 'What are you even doing here?'

'I heard a new team had come out here to try to help with the influx of people crossing the border. They said it might be a good place to start setting up a new transit camp so I thought I might as well bring a section and repair the old jenny at the same time.'

'You've dealt with the rebels back at Luerina?'

'They were well gone by the time we got there.' Hayden shrugged. 'We patrolled as far as we could with the local police but there was no sign of them. For now, we have to assume they got what they wanted and left, though the police are still up there, trying to stay on hand in case anywhere else gets hit.'

He stood up and moved to stand next to her, and she could feel the heat pouring off his wide, solid chest. Her body went into overdrive, though she tried to pretend to herself that it hadn't.

'And when you've finished playing superman here?'

'Then I'm going to check on the rest of my guys. They're building our first permanent bridge a few clicks away. The components got parachuted in last night.'

'I heard on the radio.' She laughed. 'Apparently the whole camp is buzzing about it. I heard all the kids ran out to the drop zone and you guys had to widen your perimeter fence?'

'Yeah, got a bit hairy for a while, but it was all good. If you're ready to get back to Jukrem tonight, can you give us another few hours? I'd really like to get this pump working properly again for them.'

Technically she was due back to ensure cover for the next shift, but she knew Mandy would rather wait a little longer if it meant the people of this village could regain access to clean, fresh water. Besides, there were so many potential patients to see that she definitely wouldn't be short of work.

'I can give you a little while,' she replied.

'That's all I'll need.'

He was already dropping back to the ground when she heard the roar of an engine as his second-in-command headed towards them at speed. The vehicle slowed down far enough away not to put any of the crowding villagers in danger, but as Dean jumped down and began running over, Bridget knew it was serious. No one ran in this heat unless there was a damned good reason.

Her stomach began to swan-dive.

Especially when Hayden stood abruptly and hurried to the captain. Close enough that she could hear them but far enough that the rest of the crowd couldn't.

'What's going on, Dean?'

'Conversation with the project coordinator,' Dean imparted. 'Message in on the charity radio is that Lawian village has just been hit by the renegades. Probably the same group that hit Lu-erina.'

For a moment, she had to think where Lawian was. A satellite clinic in a small town northeast of Jukrem and southeast of the main city and charity camp in Rejupe.

'Casualties?' Hayden asked.

'No serious casualties, just been roughed up a bit. However, some shots were fired.'

'Okay, so they're really moving around, and

that's also an escalation,' Hayden said, waving her over. 'Did you catch all that, Birdie?'

She nodded grimly, hurrying over.

'Last time they just waved the guns in the villagers' faces and beeped horns.'

'Anything else?' Hayden asked Dean.

'Yeah, everything Mandy has gleaned suggests that they are heading south and they're getting more desperate.'

'Do we know if they're heading to us?' Hayden asked, his eyes flickering to her for a split second, and her heart gave a tiny leap at the idea that his instinct might have been concern for her.

Even if he'd then pushed it aside and focused on his task in hand, as he was meant to do.

'We've no way of knowing if the bandits are going to keep coming south, or if they'll veer off more southeast when they realise that we're in the area. *We* as in the British Army.' Dean swiftly turned to her. 'Not *we* as in your charity.'

'I understand that,' she assured him. 'What about the local police? Didn't you just say they were patrolling in case anywhere else got hit?'

'I said they were still patrolling up north of Rejupe,' Hayden confirmed. 'We didn't anticipate the rebels moving so far or so fast. If they hit Laiwan, that would make the police one or two days out by now.'

'Which is why they're hoping we can help,' Dean added.

'We might not need to do much more than look menacing,' Hayden said thoughtfully. 'The criminals are hitting small villages that can't really protect themselves, stealing what they can but leaving before anyone can get to them. It doesn't seem likely they'll attack this camp with us being so close by.'

'I thought the same thing,' Dean confirmed. 'Our mere presence might be enough to make them stay away.'

'We can hope.' Hayden looked grim. 'For now let's keep it between us and Mandy, no need to alert the rest of the staff and panic anyone. But is she prepared to evacuate the staff on short notice, like Camp Luerina did?'

Again his gaze flickered to her, as if he couldn't help himself. Dean, mercifully, didn't seem to notice.

'Mandy wants your assessment before she makes her recommendation, sir.'

Bridget opened her mouth to argue then closed it again. The charity would be legally obliged to err on the side of caution, but none of the staff would want to leave. But better to let Mandy tell Hayden that they would be staying put—after all she was the project coordinator.

Besides, that wasn't what was playing on her mind the most. The simple fact was that last time, back at Rejupe, she'd been daunted enough by the prospect of him heading out to face rebels, but she'd managed to quash it. She'd managed to convince herself that this was his job, just as the nursing was hers.

But this time, somehow, it was different. Perhaps because Dean had already confirmed that the scale of the attacks was escalating, and she knew that would put Hayden and his guys into greater danger.

It made it all the more real. All the more frightening. As she could lose him.

As if she was in a position to lose him.

'Okay,' Hayden decided, making her jump slightly as she listened to his commands to his captain. 'Let's put out a warning order to the guys to prep for escorting the charity vehicles in any potential emergency evacuation.'

Hayden began jotting down names.

All business. No time for emotion.

'They need to ready a DROPS to carry an MGB, and let's have these guys tasked with constructing that on the route out, and two four-by-fours. You're going to need to put them on driver rest so scrap any tasks they've got lined up over the next couple of days.'

'We'll want to evacuate a couple of the severely ill but stable patients that we can't afford to leave behind if we can help it,' Bridget interjected quickly.

'Mandy didn't mention it,' pointed out Dean.

'I know, but she *will* want to. I can guarantee

it.' There was nothing personal in Dean's uncertainty, Bridget knew that, but she'd worked on enough projects over the years to be confident of her facts. 'I understand you'll need to contact her for confirmation but if you could factor it in. And if you could provide any additional support in that area.'

'How many?' Hayden asked her.

Later, she would take her time mulling over the glorious fact that he hadn't questioned her, he'd merely accepted. Later, though. Not now.

'We have three four-by-fours for staff and a couple of patients. I think we'll want to bring a minimum of four more who can't be left. More, if you could accommodate them.'

'Okay.' Hayden dipped his head, adding more names to the list. 'Dean, if you can ready a second DROPS to act as an ambulance. I'm thinking Dutton and Chester to drive, charity workers in the back with the patients.'

'I'd maybe swap Dutton for Gould,' Dean recommended. 'Dutton pulled some kind of injury doing some groundworks yesterday. Not serious but I'd rather have another second driver.'

'Fine. And speak to Carl, the infantry platoon commander, about picking a section to escort.'

'Will do. I'll head back now. Are you on your way?'

'My guys will finish up here and then we'll

head out,' Hayden confirmed, handing his second-in-command the list of names. 'And, Dean, best let the embassy know.'

CHAPTER FOURTEEN

THE TENT WAS ROASTING. Packed with jostling bodies and feverish conversation. But everyone fell silent the instant Hayden walked in, flanked by Dean and Mandy.

'Okay, guys, as you're all aware there have been escalating attacks on several of the villages in the region,' Hayden began without preamble. 'You'll need to prepare for an emergency evacuation to Rejupe and the army will offer support.'

'What about the patients?' Bridget asked at once, her eyes on Mandy for fear that she'd give herself away if she looked at Hayden.

'It has been decided that you'll take the most serious of the patients only,' Hayden answered instead.

As one, the medical staff all turned to Mandy, waiting for her to argue the case for staying. The refugees needed them. But uncharacteristically Mandy was silent.

'How bad was the attack?' Lisa demanded

after a moment. 'You're the army. Can't you guys fight them off?'

Bridget tried not to look at Hayden, but the draw was too strong.

'We were sent here to build infrastructure for the surrounding area, not as a fighting force. We didn't anticipate any hostile activity and we don't have authorisation to engage them. You need to get ready to evacuate.'

'We can't just leave,' Lisa argued. 'Mandy, please. You can't want us to leave?'

'I do understand how you feel,' the older woman replied empathetically. 'Really, I do. But it isn't a risk the charity can afford to take. I'll need most of you to be ready to leave in the first wave back to Rejupe if necessary, taking the most critical patients and as much kit as we can.'

'We can't just leave the rest of the patients,' Bridget pointed out. 'They still need our care.'

'We'll keep a small group here—I'll be one of them—to keep things ticking over,' Mandy confirmed. 'But if things get too dangerous, we'll have to leave, too.'

As if they truly just thought this was a genuine, if tense back and forth between colleagues.

'But we have a troop of Royal Engineers,' someone said. 'As well as a detachment of infantry a couple of hundred metres away. Surely these renegades would have to be crazy to attack us?'

Mandy nodded and shrugged all at once.

'All the more reason to believe that they're getting more and more desperate if they're heading down this way, knowing all of that.'

'And desperate groups are unpredictable groups,' Hayden added. 'We can't assume they won't get desperate enough to kidnap and ransom a charity worker.'

'And if they shoot you?' someone asked, from the back of the tent.

'Well, in that case we have the right to engage.' He paused, then clarified, 'To fire back.'

But Bridget was already gripping the metal table behind her, trying to stop this sensation that she was suddenly free-falling into nothingness.

If the rebels shot at Hayden and his men, it changed the parameters. How had she not realised that before? There would be a gunfight… or what had he called it? A firefight? It wasn't unrealistic to consider that he might get injured.

Killed.

Nausea raced to meet her.

She was an idiot. She'd let herself get too close to him. Too invested. Despite everything she'd told herself. And now she was terrified he was going to confront a group of rebels and he could get hurt.

Worse.

Yet this was his job. It was what he did. What he *loved* doing. She had no right to wish that she could stop him. No right to wish that he would want stay…with her.

'Can't you build a compound around this facility?' She fought to drag her mind back the present.

'We can, but in this short time it won't be big enough, or secure enough, to encompass all the medical tents, the new generators, and all the *tukul* accommodation.'

Her stomach pulled tight and twisted as she listened to all the voices.

'Meaning?'

'Meaning we need to keep it compact and just incorporate the most necessary areas and a skeleton staff, who also need to be ready to evacuate on command.'

Bridget had no idea how she managed to tear her gaze from his, but somehow she managed to slide her eyes to Mandy.

'Fine. Then I'm volunteering to be one of the staff who stays behind.'

'No.'

His voice cracked out around the room. She could hardly breathe. She certainly couldn't face him. He sounded so cold. So hard. She opened her mouth to argue but nothing came out. Not that he gave her the opportunity in any case.

'I can't allow staff to decide for themselves who evacuates to the main hospital now and who remains in camp. As project chief, Mandy and I have discussed all staff in terms of medical capabilities as well as previous experience in the potential risk voluntary confinement camps such as this one will become.'

It was all Bridget could do not to reel at the force in his tone. She understood that this was his job, but it didn't explain his brusque attitude. As though he somehow blamed her for something.

Her head ached, trying to work it out.

Perhaps he thought the night with her had stopped him from seeing something earlier? Acting to stop the rebels. Although she didn't see how that could make sense.

But what else could account for this sudden, awful hostility?

It was like her heart was cracking in her chest and every word was being ripped from her mouth, and yet her colleagues seemed utterly oblivious to the undercurrents between her and Hayden.

'We've unanimously agreed a list of five names. Don't bother arguing, Nurse, your name isn't on it, and you'll be wasting everybody's time.'

'Actually...' Mandy spoke up, her eyes scanning her notes, seemingly equally unaware of the undertones. 'I could do with you staying,

Bridget. You went through this kind of scenario a few years ago, didn't you?'

'I did.' Bridget nodded, keeping her gaze firmly away from Hayden, even though she could feel his eyes boring into her.

It was the oddest sensation.

'Good, okay, I'll add your name.' Mandy scribbled her name on the page before nodding her confirmation to Hayden.

Was she the only one who could feel his disapproval bouncing around the room? And yet, like the soldier that she'd known, he quashed it before he spoke.

'All right, the staff staying back will be briefed by Mandy now to prep any patients the first wave will be taking with them in this initial evacuation.'

There wasn't even a low grumble of protest as the group, evidently jolted by Hayden's unequivocal tone, moved forward to check the list.

'The rest of you have ten minutes to grab your personal gear and get back here to collect those patients. The transport will be leaving in half an hour and nobody will be late, are we clear?'

'Clear,' came the chorus as people checked the list and then spilled out of the tent to carry out their designated roles.

But as Bridget headed off, she wasn't prepared for Hayden to snag her arm, pulling her into one of the *tukuls* under repair the moment no one was watching.

Her heart hammered against her ribcage. Whatever this was about, she didn't think it was going to be good.

'You need to remove your name from the volunteers staying behind.'

He shouldn't be doing this, he knew that, and yet he hadn't been able to help himself. And now, even as Bridget blinked at him, her lovely eyes looking hurt, he hated himself in a way he never had done in his life before.

But he didn't relent.

He couldn't.

This was the right call for the right reasons, wasn't it?

Hayden stared grimly across the *tukul* and into a face he was sure would haunt him forever. He had never—in his entire career—had to second-guess his motivations before. He didn't like it.

But he was forced to concede that he liked even less the idea of anything happening to Bridget.

'Remove your name, Birdie,' his voice rasped out.

Her brow furrowed and Hayden found himself clenching his fists to stop himself from reaching out and smoothing it flat.

'Why?'

'Because it's not safe.'

She eyed him with astonishment for a moment, before she bit back.

'It's a lot safer than what you're doing.'

'I don't care.' It was all he could do to keep his voice down, knowing all too well how sound carried out here. 'You can't stay here.'

'Why not?'

He didn't want to answer. Yet he couldn't not. Everything in him was railing at what he was doing but he didn't care. He had to stop her. He had to keep her safe.

'Because you're a liability.' He barely recognised the sound of his own voice.

He hardly blamed her for looking at him with shock. Then horror. Then fury.

'I'm a what?'

'You're a liability,' he repeated, even if through his teeth.

This wasn't him. This wasn't what he did. And yet here he was, unable to help himself.

'I am *not* a liability,' she managed to hiss, though there was no mistaking the shake in her voice. 'I am *very* good at my job.'

'You're a liability to *me*.'

Everything froze around him. The hut. The camp. The world. It was just him and her, and for a split second he wished it was all there would ever be.

'Say that again?' she whispered.

He didn't know if he couldn't or if he just didn't want to. It was an admission he hadn't imagined he would ever make. But the moment he heard it he realised the truth.

He cared for this woman. In a way he'd never thought he'd ever care for anyone. A part of him had realised it earlier, of course. A few days ago? A week ago? Longer?

Hayden didn't know. He just knew that he couldn't stand the thought of anything happening to her. Ever.

'You heard me,' he bit out instead.

For a moment he thought he saw a flicker of... something in her expression before she shut it down.

'I'm a liability?' she asked softly. 'To you?'

'Forget it. Just withdraw your name.'

'Because you care about me.' It was less of a question and more of a realisation, and yet he couldn't answer her. 'Say it, Hayd. Tell me you care.'

And the sickest part was that even though a part of him wanted to tell her—desperately—he refused to. As if that could somehow make this moment, this *weakness* disappear.

'I don't care.'

'Clearly you do.'

'No,' he denied, despite that fact that even *he* didn't believe himself. 'No more than I care about any of your colleagues. I just don't need the distraction.'

'If you don't care, why am I any more of a distraction than anyone else?'

Everything tumbled within him. This churning sea of...*feelings* he had never had to deal with before. Had never wanted to.

He was cool and detached. He prided himself on it. He didn't drag other people into his life because it was never steady or consistent enough. Hadn't his kind, caring but permanently unsettled mother taught him that much?

'This is your job, Hayden.' Bridget was speaking suddenly. Her voice was firmer than he thought he'd heard before. 'And it frightens me, what you do, but I accept it. It's who you are and it's what makes you tick. But nursing out here is who *I* am. This is what makes *me* proud of who I am. And you have no right to ask me to stop that because you've suddenly realised you care for me.'

'That isn't what this is about,' he growled.

'I think it is.'

'Remove your name, Birdie,' he bit out. 'Or I will go to Mandy and do it for you.'

And then, before he could betray his own code of ethics any further, he swung around and left the hut.

And the woman that he was terribly afraid he was beginning to love.

Bridget waited for the helicopter to come in to Rejupe on a rare, miserable, overcast day, and pretended it didn't feel portentous.

She'd asked Mandy for the transfer the moment their small team had been evacuated from Jukremafter all. There were any number of the charity's other camps in the region that were far enough away to be safe from the rebels and which were crying out for an extra pair of hands. Some of the Jukrem camp staff were filling in gaps in the main Rejupe compound, whilst others, like her, were transferring out to smaller camps across the area.

It was no big deal, she told herself crossly as she commanded her hands and body to stop shaking. When they didn't obey, she tried telling herself that it was anger.

She suspected it was more grief.

Up to that moment in the *tukul* a few nights ago, she'd been afraid that Hayden hated her. That he was trying to shut her out and disengage from her. And the idea of him pulling away from her had hurt more than she'd ever wanted to admit.

But the truth seemed to be that he didn't hate her, he *loved* her in his own way, and impossibly, devastatingly that was worse. Because his idea of love was dominance and control. Just like her father had dominated her mother. Hayden didn't believe in equity or mutual compassion. He believed in her supporting him in his career, but him dictating what she chose to do in her life.

And the worst of it was that she had realised she was so in love with him that a part of her had actually considered taking her name off the list that night. Even if she'd only entertained the notion for a moment.

But, then, that wasn't love at all, was it?

It couldn't be. Which was why she had to leave.

All she needed now was for Mandy to get the final paperwork signed off for her to take with her on the flight, and in a few hours she'd be over one hundred miles away in another village, another camp, where she wouldn't run into Hayden Brigham.

It might not be a decision that her heart liked, but it was a logical decision. Her best choice, given the circumstances. She could complete the remaining months of her programme without her heart being constantly in her mouth in case she walked out of the clinic and turned the corner, only to walk into him.

How impossible would it be to keep focused on her job as she should—as she had always been able to do in the past—when a hopeless part of her was anticipating the next time they would be alone.

When her traitorous body kept reminding her what it felt like to be with him—the only man who had ever truly known her. And how it would feel again?

She stood up rapidly, pacing the bare room as if that could somehow dislodge the image of him that had pinned itself to her brain. That thatch of dirty blond hair. His dimpled chin. The chiselled body.

She picked up the pace abruptly, and she told herself that was relief she could feel spiralling through her. Not something that felt dangerously like something else entirely.

It had been a mistake to let herself get too close to him. Hayden had warned her from the start, but she hadn't listened to him. She'd been too caught up in the…the *feelings* sloshing around inside her. Her inexperience, she supposed, in mistaking sex for emotions. Believing that their nights together—even their conversations—had meant more to him than they had.

That *she* had meant more to him than she had.

But there was no escaping the truth of it. The sexual chemistry between them—so powerful that it was almost self-destructive—was just that. *Sexual chemistry.* Not a connection, or bonding, and certainly not *love*. Which was why she couldn't go back to Jukrem.

Bridget held her hand to her chest as if the action could still the fluttering in her chest. Jukrem meant Hayden. And her weakness. They were bound to end up back in bed together, probably more than once, if she returned. The offer to take up a role at another camp couldn't have come at a better time, she reminded herself for the tenth time in the past hour.

She heard Mandy's footsteps in the dirt long before the project coordinator rounded the corner. Making herself stop pacing, Bridget adopted what she hoped was a wide, bright smile.

'Everything ready?'

'Not exactly.'

There was no way to stop her stomach from rolling and soaring, try as she did to rein it in.

'Hayd.' Her voice didn't sound remotely even. 'I was expecting Mandy. When did you get here?'

'About five minutes ago,' he growled.

'And the rebels?'

She wasn't quite sure how she even remembered them, her head felt so thick and muggy.

'Caught. Local enforcement arrived last night.' He waved his hand irritably. 'I didn't come here to talk to you about some low-level criminals.'

'Well, it's what I want to talk about.' Not true in its strictest sense. But it was certainly the only thing she was *prepared* to talk about. 'There are so many patients still to treat in Jukrem, it's good to know the rest of the volunteers can return.'

'You can *all* return.'

'I won't be going.'

He cast her an exasperated look. And…something more. Something she didn't care to examine too closely, lest it sway her from her goal of leaving.

'You can't be serious about taking up a position at another camp?'

'Why not?' Smoothing her hands over her dusty combat trousers, Bridget tried to remind herself of everything she'd been saying earlier. Only it was rapidly sliding from her head. 'I've been offered the position of selecting and training a healthcare team of locals. It's a promotion.'

'You're one of the medical staff. Not admin.'

'That doesn't mean I can't be given a more responsible role.' Her voice cracked, and she stopped abruptly. 'Plus, this means I get to extend my assignment for a further three months. I gain more experience in this environment, which can only be good for my career.'

He sounded so disapproving. So dismissive. She needed a moment to compose herself, but he was already snapping out alternatives.

Commands. As though he thought he knew better.

'Ask Mandy for more responsibility at Jukrem. After everything you did on that emergency run last month, and the evacuation the other day, you've proved yourself to be one of the most valuable members the team has. And Jukrem is where you're meant to be stationed anyway.'

Her chest was pulling so tight she expected to hear her ribs crack any moment. He was doing it again—telling her what he thought was best. Expecting her to agree because he'd said it? Again, exactly as her father had done.

So how was it possible to want, so badly, to agree to what Hayden was saying? She hated herself for being so weak.

'I'm not staying, Hayden,' she managed to bite out suddenly.

She didn't know where it came from, but she clung to it nonetheless.

'You have to stay,' he stated. The hint of barely disguised bleakness in his tone made her heart fracture. 'If you leave...'

She didn't want to answer, but she couldn't help herself.

'If I leave...?'

'If you leave, how will I know that you're okay? That you're safe?'

The admission hung, shimmering, in the air between them. So ethereal that she was afraid that if she reached out to touch it, it would disappear, never to have existed in the first instance.

'Hayd...' she began at length, before stalling.

He began moving again, so slowly that at first that she didn't even realise it until he came to a halt in front of her.

And then he reached out, his hand hovering millimetres from her cheek, making her want to lean into him. She would never know how she resisted.

'Hayd…' Her voice was barely more than a whisper, but that was all she could manage. 'I don't understand any of this. A few days ago, you were telling me I had to leave because you were mad you couldn't focus with me around. Now you're telling me I have to stay so that you know I'm okay. You must see how wrong that is.'

'To want you to be safe?' He let out a hollow laugh. 'I'm sure that's very wrong.'

'No.' She kept her voice even though she didn't know how. 'To ask me to run my life according to what works for *you*.'

'That isn't what I said,' he refuted.

Still, he let his hand drop, the frankness in his gravelly tone jolting through her. It made her forget, for a moment, everything she'd in which just been schooling herself. Every caution.

'Yes. It is.'

And the worst of it was that a part of her wanted to obey, as long as that meant being with him. Building something with him.

But what could they possibly build that could be real under those circumstances?

'I know the army is your career, your life. It's what you love. And I respect that. But the nursing, and this charity, is what I love. And you don't respect *that*.'

''I was keeping you safe the only way I knew how,' he ground out, and disappointment roared through her.

'Then you should have found another way than expecting me to fall in with everything you wanted. It wasn't fair. It wasn't professional consideration. It wasn't mutual recognition.'

'What did you expect?' he asked harshly. 'For me to tell you to crack on and stay until things got really close to the wire? Or for me to beg you to leave in the first wave because I didn't want you hurt and that I loved you?'

'Do you love me?' she asked abruptly.

'Do you think loving someone means choosing them over your job? Your career?'

Of course he wasn't going to answer her. She'd known it even as she'd asked the question. But suddenly the truth enveloped her, like a sandstorm, harsh and unrelenting. *She* loved *him*. She might have never really experienced it before but that didn't mean she didn't *know*. Besides, there was nothing else that this deep, roaring, all-consuming *thing* inside her could be.

Love.

Painful and beautiful.

But wholly unrequited.

Still, she didn't know how she broke contact, taking a less than steady step backwards.

'That wasn't what I was asking. And, for the record, I think a person can have both.' She barely recognised her own discordant voice. 'And I'm going to the new camp.'

'Bridget…'

She straightened her shoulders, hitherto unknown strength beginning to flow through her. Sluggish and reluctant, but there nonetheless.

'I have to go. For me. Not for anyone else and certainly not for you. I want to do something for me. Can you understand that?'

She turned, barely able think straight, but in the instant before she looked away she was sure that she saw him take pause for a moment.

Or, probably, it was some perverse wishful thinking on her part. The silence stretched out for what felt like an eternity and then, finally, he answered.

'I can understand it.' His voice rasped over her. 'Have a safe flight, Bridget. They'll be lucky to have you.'

'Thanks.' Her throat was so constricted she could barely answer.

And then Hayden walked away—as her silly, insubstantial dreams floated down around her like ashes.

CHAPTER FIFTEEN

'I CAN'T BELIEVE you're advocating that I leave the army,' his sister snorted at him as she sat, upright with back straight, at the kitchen table in their father's home. 'You were the one who told me—repeatedly—that I was crazy for giving it up for George. But you think it's okay to give it up for Kane?'

Did he think that?

Hayden faltered. For the first time in his life he wasn't one hundred percent sure what he thought. His head was all over the place and it was all to do with the woman who was still thousands of miles away right now.

Bridget.

It didn't matter how far away she was, she was nonetheless haunting every one of his thoughts.

He'd been so caught up in his own astonishing hubris, and the paralysing fear that something could happen to her out there that he hadn't accepted what she'd been saying even as she'd said it.

In that one idiotic move he'd effectively asked her to turn her back on her passion and her goals, the things that made her *her*. The things that had made him fall for her in the first place.

He would never have entertained any woman who had demanded those things of him. In fact, he *hadn't* entertained them, and they *had* tried it.

There was an indisputable irony in that fact that didn't pass him by.

'No,' he heard himself answering slowly. Reminding himself where he was and who he was talking to. 'I think it's crazy to give up something you love for anyone else but yourself.'

And it was gradually dawning on him that although he was speaking aloud to his sister, in the kitchen of his childhood home, in his mind he might as well have been saying the same exact words to Bridget.

He could see Mattie turning to stare at him, no doubt wondering who he was and what he'd done with the brother she knew. Or *had known*, right up until Bridget had walked into his life. The least he owed his sister was to answer her questions, but instead of with his head he'd be answering with his heart.

'Be that George, Kane or the Queen of England—and you take the Queen's shilling every pay cheque. My point is that you can blame others as much as you like for not telling you the truth back then, but you've had a chance to put things right—if that's what you really want—and you've decided to stick with the devil you know. And that's on you, Mattie. No one else.'

Just as it was on him to put things right with Bridget, Hayden thought, turning around to pick up his sister's freshly brewed mug of tea and pass it to her.

He watched her cup it in her hands and slide her fingers through the handle, glowering at him over the rim. And still all he could think about was Bridget, and how he only had himself to blame for the way things had ended between them.

'So, what's your next assignment anyway?' Mattie asked.

'I'm supposed to be DS for a training exercise on Salisbury Plain.'

A few months ago he would have relished this task. It had to mean something that he couldn't muster up an ounce of enthusiasm for it.

'Supposed to be?'

Mattie narrowed her eyes, but Hayden was grateful that she was too preoccupied with her own thoughts of Kane to really be concentrating on what he'd said.

The truth was that he'd rather be somewhere else than the UK entirely. Somewhere thousands of miles away. Somewhere with a certain person. It was the most bizarre sensation. Certainly not one he'd ever had to contend with before.

Who would have thought that one woman could have turned his whole life on its head this way? And it had happened so quietly, so stealthily that he hadn't seen it coming for even a second.

Bridget Gardiner.

If he wasn't to change the dialogue with her, he was going to have to find a new approach. Soon, thanks to requests from the various charity project coordinators he had met in his time out there, his CO would be sending out a new contingent to the region for ongoing support. They would carry out similar infrastructure work to that they'd carried out at Jukrem, but this time at other camps such as Rejupe, and further afield.

Only one question remained: *was he willing to*?

Snatching up one of the few remaining paediatric units of O negative from the refrigerator unit in the lab, Bridget began decanting the blood into the sterile bags for paediatric use before taking a sample in order to allow her to conduct a bedside crossmatch.

'You paged?' Justin, the doctor, hurried in as Bridget was back at the child's bedside.

By the looks of it, he had just woken from what had probably only been his first hour's sleep in about the last twenty hours.

'You look like hell,' Bridget offered by way of

apology. 'Patient is an eighteen-month-old baby, presented about ten minutes ago very pale, low oxygen, bloody diarrhoea, and a haemoglobin of two point nine.'

'How much blood have we got?' he asked grimly.

'Not a lot. But there are at least three donors out there so we'll screen them as quickly as we can.'

'Okay.' He began to examine the baby, no doubt taking in the same muscle-wasting, anaemia and malnutrition that she had. 'It's going to be hard to find a vein.'

If by *hard* he meant *basically impossible*, she concurred.

'IV line to normal saline?' she suggested.

'I knew you were here for a reason.' Justin nodded grimly. 'I know you've been on duty all night but you're the best crossmatcher we have.'

'I'm not going anywhere,' Bridget assured him, pushing back against the wall of exhaustion that threatened to crash over her.

'That's good, because the new army units are due in today.'

For a fraction of a second Bridget froze. And then she threw herself into her task, but this time the wall threatening to crash over her wasn't one of exhaustion but of memories—forceful but unwelcome. Thinking of the new army units arriving made her think about Hayd, whom she couldn't think about without her chest feeling as though an entire herd of elephants was sitting on it, crushing it.

What made it all the more laughable was the fact that the charity had only decided to extend its working relationship with the British Army because they'd been so impressed with how well the relationship had worked in Jukrem.

Now other medical camps in the region were getting Royal Engineers to work on infrastructure, whilst the relationship between Hayden and herself had died a pitiful death.

And still an even more foolish part of her had half imagined that now Operation Ironplate was over for him, Hayden might have tried to come out on one of the new charity/army operations, this time in her area. But he hadn't, and she hated herself for that traitorous voice stirring things up.

She hated herself even more for the other voice that told her it was merely telling the truth.

Four months, and she still hadn't learned. But volunteering out here had always brought one thing back to her more than anything else. Life was too short for grudges.

She was still cross-matching the first patient when one of their colleagues rushed in.

'Another emergency on its way. A two-year-old girl with high fever, suffering convulsions and diarrhoea. Haemoglobin three point one.

Preliminary assessment in the clinic is that it's malaria.'

'Another IV line,' Justin confirmed. 'Intramuscular injections, and malaria tablets, and, Bridget...?'

'More cross-matching.' Bridget nodded. 'Got it. Is her mother in with her?'

'Yes. I'll take her to the lab for screening,' the nurse assured them, hurrying back to the door. Then turned. 'Also, the new army unit has arrived. They've already started investigating the pump in the south quarter so we might even have additional fresh water by nightfall.'

It was the kind of thing Hayden would have done, Bridget couldn't help thinking. He would have launched himself into emergency tasks like that. If they succeeded, the limit of five litres per person per day could be raised to ten litres. Still less than the ideal minimum of fifteen litres out here, but quite an improvement for a few hours' work.

But it hadn't happened yet.

Thrusting the thoughts away, she focused on the two cross-matches over the next couple of hours, as well as third one that came in, only feeling she could breathe again when the life-saving blood was being transfused into all three of their tiny patients.

At last, exhausted yet with an enormous sense of satisfaction, Bridget called her shift done and left the medical part of the compound and headed for the mess tent to grab a bit of rather late lunch.

'I didn't think you'd ever come out.'

Whatever tiredness or hunger had been threatening to overtake her, it dissipated in that instant. Slowly she turned, half expecting him to be a mirage. That he'd disappear when she tried to look directly at him.

'Hayd. What are you doing here?'

'New orders,' he told her easily, but she didn't miss that expression in his gaze.

The one that caught at her, tugging on the loose thread until it threatened to unravel. She commanded herself not to react.

'New orders?'

'To check the boreholes. Strip down and rebuild any of the submersible electric pumps that need it. Get them working again.'

'I knew there was an army unit coming.' She was impressed with herself at how steady her voice sounded. She had no idea how she'd managed it. 'I just didn't think for a moment that it would be you. Is that a coincidence?'

Hayden's eyes slammed into hers so hard she felt as though he had physically winded her.

'No, Birdie, it isn't a coincidence.' His voice rolled through her like thunder. Like a prelude to the monsoon season that wasn't yet due. 'I put in a request to my CO to come out here, to be part of this follow-up mission, because I wanted to see you. I missed you.'

She wanted to believe him. So much that her heart felt like it was cracking. But something lurked in the periphery of her mind. A dark shadow that warned her not to be as gullible and foolish as her mother had always been.

Hadn't he already told her he couldn't offer her any kind of relationship? So what had changed?

'You missed the sex.' She hated the sound of every single word, yet they had to be said. 'Nothing more.'

'No, I missed you,' he corrected, reaching out to take one loose lock of black hair in his fingers and twirl it.

The tiny gesture felt so intimate that it almost stole her breath away. If she didn't steel her heart against him she was afraid he was going to shatter it all over again. But it still didn't explain what had changed in his head.

'You don't,' she refuted thickly. 'And I don't want to go down this road with you again.'

And then, before she could crumble, as she feared she surely would, Bridget found the strength to remove his hand and begin to walk away.

Whilst she still could.

'I was wrong,' he said quietly. Simply.

And she knew she shouldn't engage with him,

but she couldn't help it. She stopped, but she didn't turn around.

'I don't know what that means.'

'It means I want more.'

The softly spoken words hung there in the dry, hot midday air. And Bridget didn't know which of them would reach for them first. Slowly, very slowly, she turned around, murmuring, 'Say that again?'

'You heard me the first time,' he answered, but there was no rancour to his tone.

This time when he approached her and reached for her, she couldn't bring herself to pull away.

More to the point, she didn't want to.

'More?'

'A lot more.'

Yet it wasn't the words that got under her skin—or, at least, it wasn't *only* the words—it was also that stunned, raw expression in his gaze that was her undoing. It made her throat parched and her voice scratchy.

And it also made her oddly, perhaps irrationally, angry.

'You suddenly decide you want more? You come haring up here on some pretext of a reassignment? And you expect me to drop everything and welcome you with open arms?'

'You think I'm going to change my mind,' he stated clearly. Empathetically.

She was *terrified* he would change his mind.

But she didn't need to tell him that, not least because she was still trying to process what he'd said.

'I don't *think* you'll change your mind. I fully *expect* that you will,' she shot back. 'Because, no matter what you say now, your career comes first with you. Just as mine does with me.'

'There's no reason why we can't have both.' He lifted his hands to cup her cheeks. 'A wise woman once told me that, only I wasn't ready to listen to her.'

Bridget told herself that she wanted to pull away.

Only she didn't. Not a millimetre. She just stayed right where she was, her eyes locked with Hayden's and her feet rooted in place.

'And now you *are* ready?' she asked a little breathlessly.

He shot her a look she could only describe as solemn.

'For the rest of my life,' he assured her.

'The rest of your life?' she echoed, almost in wonder.

This all felt very real, and yet wholly unreal. It couldn't be happening to her, surely?

'The rest of *our* lives,' Hayden corrected. 'You only have to say you'll take me back.'

She wasn't entirely sure it was a request. It sounded more like a command, albeit couched in the softest terms. Yet it was a command she felt she could obey.

For the first time since she'd walked outside she smiled.

How could it be that her smile shone brighter than the equatorial sun? And seared him twice as strongly?

He'd never dreamt he'd ever find a woman like Bridget, who made him feel complete when he hadn't known he'd even been broken. He'd spent years congratulating himself that he hadn't fallen into the same relationship trap that friends and colleagues alike had fallen into. One night with Bridget and he'd stepped right into it and had never even realised it.

'I'm not a man of words, Birdie,' he told her apologetically. 'I'm usually a man of action. I don't know how to tell you what you've come to mean to me, but I hoped by coming up here with my team it would prove it to you instead.'

'I think I'd like both,' she told him with a half-laugh.

She was probably joking, yet because she'd asked, something inside him wanted to try; wanted to be the kind of man who could tell her what was in his heart.

'Okay.' He held her. 'How about this? I've spent all my life ducking the idea of settling with one person. Believing that it was better to be like this than give any woman the life my father gave my mother. However much she loved him.'

'Hayd—' she began, but he dropped his lips to hers and momentarily silenced her.

A mere brush of their lips, yet it was enough to almost send him over the edge.

'I think I loved you the moment you walked into that damned nightclub with my sister as your personal bodyguard.'

'Was it the danger of being attracted to your kid sister's friend?' She grinned, but he could see the hint of uncertainty in her and he loved the fact that he could read her even when she was trying to cover herself.

'No.' He shook his head, his eyes dangerously sexy. 'It was most definitely not that. It was the danger of *you*, Birdie. Pure and simple. I couldn't resist.'

'You certainly made me think you were going to,' she teased.

'I've no idea how,' he groaned, stepping forward and gripping her shoulders. Not tightly enough to hurt but enough to hold her in place and make sure she was listening. 'It damned near killed me, Birdie, and I never want to have to do that again.'

'Is that so?'

'That's so,' he confirmed. 'One month in your company and I realised that what was *really* better was to find a woman who actually wanted to live the life that I did.'

He loved the way her eyes glittered, like crystals of demerara sugar dropped into the richest, darkest pools of strong coffee.

'But not always, Hayd.' She pursed her lips ruefully. 'What about in the future?'

'I don't know what the future will hold. I only know that I don't want to face it unless I'm by your side. You and I. Together.'

'You should know now that I want a family one day. Maybe that will be ten years from now. But one day.'

'I want that too, with you,' he told her, knowing that there wasn't a part of him that doubted it. He wanted everything with her. Now he understood what Mattie had been going on about.

And then, before either of them could waste any more breath talking about it, he lowered his head and claimed her mouth with his own.

The first kiss of the rest of their lives.

* * * * *